War of
The Worlds

War of
The Worlds

Jay Dubya

BOOKSTAND
PUBLISHING
ESTD. 2006
www.bookstandpublishing.com

Published by
Bookstand Publishing
Pasadena, CA 91101
4947_7

Cover design and front cover illustration by Al Margolis

ISBN 978-1-956785-45-6

For Steve and Michelle

Other Books by Jay Dubya

Adult Fiction

Black Leather and Blue Denim, A '50s Novel
The Great Teen Fruit War, A 1960' Novel
Frat' Brats, A '60s Novel
Ron Coyote, Man of La Mangia
Pieces of Eight
Pieces of Eight, Part II
Pieces of Eight, Part III
Pieces of Eight, Part IV
The Wholly Book of Genesis
The Wholly Book of Exodus
The Wholly Book of Doo-Doo-Rot-on-Me
Thirteen Sick Tasteless Classics
Thirteen Sick Tasteless Classics, Part II
Thirteen Sick Tasteless Classics, Part III
Thirteen Sick Tasteless Classics, Part IV
Thirteen Sick Tasteless Classics, Part V
So Ya' Wanna' Be A Teacher
RAM: Random Articles and Manuscripts
Mauled Maimed Mangled Mutilated Mythology
Fractured Frazzled Folk Fables and Fairy Farces
FFFF&FF, Part II
Nine New Novellas
Nine New Novellas, Part II
Nine New Novellas, Part III
Nine New Novellas, Part IV
One Baker's Dozen
Two Baker's Dozen
Shakespeare: Slammed, Smeared, Savaged & Slaughtered
Shakespeare: Slammed, Smeared, Savaged & Slaughtered, Part II
Suite 16
Time Travel Tales
Snake Eyes and Boxcars
Snake Eyes and Boxcars, Part II
UFO: Utterly Fantastic Occurrences

The Psychic Dimension
The Psychic Dimension, Part II
Modern Mythology
First Person Stories
O. Henry: Obscenely and Outrageously Obliterated
Twain: Tattered Trounced Tortured and Traumatized
Poe: Pelted Pounded Pummeled and Pulverized
London: Lashed Lacerated Lampooned and Lambasted
Hawthorne: Hazed Hooked Hammered and Hijacked
Hawthorne Hacked, Shakespeare Sacked & Thurber Thwacked
THEMES
PLOTS
PLOTS, Part II
The FBI Inspector
Prime-Time Crime Time
The Arcane Arcade
Thirteen Tantalizing Tales
The Timeless Time Machine
Homer's Odd Sea Odyssey
HOMER'S ILL ILIAD

Young Adult Fantasy Novels

Pot of Gold
Enchanta
Space Bugs, Earth Invasion
The Eighteen Story Gingerbread House

Content Chapters

Introduction

War *of the Worlds* is adult satirical literature featuring adult language and adult situations. The setting is Maybury Hill, a suburb of London, England, around 1894, just before the turn of a new century, and also, right during the exciting advances of modern science and technology, which were dominant in the minds of people throughout the Western World.

Herbert George Wells (1866-1946) was born in England, and by the turn of the twentieth century, became one of the Founding Fathers of science fiction. Wells' most famous novels are *The Time Machine*, *War of the Worlds* and *The Invisible Man*, which were written and published between 1895 and 1905.

H.G. Wells was a great student of history, and loved thinking about mankind's ultimate destiny. In his classic stories, Wells often tells through his characters what he believes is wrong with civilization, so that's why the author never ran out of characters for his popular novels.

By mentally taking his readers into the future, or by analyzing society in the present, Herbert George Wells skillfully demonstrates exactly where the human race would be evolving unless science, culture, and emotional growth would change their present courses. Herein lies a new adult-oriented satirical version of H.G. Wells' famous short novel, *War of the Worlds*.

Introduction

Chapter 1

"THE EVE OF THE WAR"

If the dumb-ass humans comfortably living here on Planet Earth were the only intelligent life in the whole Universe, including our miniature Solar System and our much more impressive Milky Way Galaxy, then we would indeed be quite important and rightfully relevant. But only a complete idiot (and actually, a full-blown narcissistic asshole) would make such a fully bizarre assumption, or radically insane speculation.

No one with half-a-brain would have believed in the last years of the nineteenth century that this picayune world of ours was being scrupulously observed by weird-looking alien shits possessing intelligences and academic technologies decisively greater than man's inferior development. And yet, that foreign, bizarre, alien civilization had been inhabited for eons by covetous creatures, even more fucked-up than we ordinary human dipshits happen to be.

And as apathetic men and women busied themselves about their various daily psychotic, hedonistic and erotic concerns, the totally-unwary nitwits (including myself) were comprehensively being scrutinized, and also very meticulously examined from afar. Yes, we were being observed perhaps almost as narrowly as a laboratory scientist with a microscope might thoroughly perceive the transient amoeba-like creatures that abundantly swarm and multiply inside a mere drop of water.

With infinite complacency, we foolish, fucked-up men and women went scurrying about our inadvertent preoccupations all over this mediocre globe. We were casually enacting our trivial, self-righteous affairs, fully serene in our assurance of our domination over our pedestrian surroundings. It is quite possible that the chaotic microbe activity actively transpiring underneath the dedicated scientist's laboratory microscope performs in a similar tumultuous manner.

No human engaged in his or her self-important concerns ever gave a minor thought to the other worlds of infinite space as constituting any realistic source of human danger. It is curious to recall some of the mental habits of those former, idyllic, departed days enjoyed by mortal dolts all over the known Earth.

At most, asinine, terrestrial residents seldom fancied the notion that there might actually be other, more-sophisticated cultures prevalent upon Mars, and perhaps, some British boneheads even imagined that those distant civilizations on other planets might be excessively inferior to our own. Most of my fucked-up London area residents had never suspected that the alien bastards on Mars were becoming ready to aggressively assault and conquer the naïve occupants of Mother Earth.

Yet across the gulf of space, a vacuous expanse trillions of times greater than the tiny Gulf of Mexico, superior alien minds were evaluating the human race as *we* evaluate and regard earthly beasts and insects. The Red Planet schemers had been for centuries considering our demise. Those cunning Martian beings, whose advanced intellects were vast, cool, calculating and unsympathetic, had been studying this vulnerable Earth with envious eyes.

And slowly-but-surely, those extremely sophisticated alien cerebrums drew their avaricious plans against targeted mankind. And late in the nineteenth century came the great disillusionment that almost completely led to the Earth's utter destruction; a major inter-planetary military attack maliciously conceived and organized by motivated space aliens.

The planet Mars revolves about the sun at a mean distance of 140,000,000 miles, and the light and heat it receives from the sun is barely half of that intensity received by *this* world, which is 93 million miles distant from Old Sol. Mars must be, if the hypothesis has any basic truth, much older than our own fucked-up world; and long before this Earth ceased to be cooling, life upon the Martian surface must have begun its declining course into astronomical history.

The fact that Mars has much less volume than does Earth must have accelerated its quicker cooling to the temperature at which evolutionary life could have begun. Apparently, Mars at one time has (or had) sufficient air and water, along with all the other vital scientific bullshit that's necessary for the support and sustenance of animated, animal existence.

Yet, so vain and delusional happens to be modern man. And consequently, our species is so blinded by our primitive vanity, that no writer, up to the very end of the nineteenth century, ever expressed any idea that intelligent life might have evolved anywhere else in the Universe beyond its present earthly level.

Nor was it generally understood that life on Mars might be geologically much older than life on Earth, and also, quite more-remote from the sun, the standard pattern of human logic subsequently followed that Mars is not only more distant from time's beginning, but in actuality, nearer to its finite end.

The secular cooling that must someday overtake our native planet had already been virtually consummated with our neighboring world. The red planet's physical condition is still largely a mystery, but we know now that even in its equatorial region, the midday temperature on Mars is lower than the Arctic-like freeze of our most-hostile, coldest winter. Our red neighbor's air is much more attenuated than our seasonal climate patterns; its oceans have shrunken-down to the size of legendary Goliath's engorged dick, until the remaining seas now cover but a third of the planet's surface, and as its slow seasons change, huge snowcaps gather and melt about either pole, and periodically, greedily inundate its hostile temperate zones.

That last stage of atmospheric exhaustion, which to us physically and mentally weak mortals is still incredibly remote, has more-than-likely become a present-day problem for the disgruntled inhabitants of Mars. The immediate pressure of existential necessity, namely survival, had consequently brightened the fuckheads' colossal intellects; had accelerated their cerebral powers, and had hardened their avaricious hearts.

And looking across the vastness of space with their incredible instruments, such as we earthlings have scarcely dreamed of with our primitive telescopes, the Martians keenly observed, at their nearest distance of only 35,000,000 miles from our Earth, a glimmering morning star of hope, represented by *our* own warmer and inviting planet.

Earth, being green with vegetation and vastly blessed with water, and possessing a cloudy atmosphere abundant with moist fertility, must have seemed very fascinating to the Martians. Random glimpses from afar through Earth's drifting cloud cover must have exhibited broad stretches of fertile, already-populated land.

And we humans, the feckless creatures who proudly inhabit this preoccupied Earth, must have appeared to the Martians as lowly jungle monkeys might seem to our undistinguishing eyes. The intellectual side of man already admits that life is an incessant struggle for daily existence, and it would seem that this too is the belief of the unscrupulous, competitive Martian brains plotting imminent invasion.

Their mysterious world is far ahead in its evolutionary cooling, and to the contrary, this Earth of ours is still crowded with life, but populated only with what the distant schemers regarded as inferior, inadequate, rudimentary animal behavior. To carry warfare sunward, and the despicable creatures only escape from impending destruction, was to sagely plan and conduct a massive invasion and conquest of their neighboring blue planet.

And before we judge the overzealous scoundrels too harshly, we must remember what ruthless and utter destruction that our own species has wrought upon our life-giving environment, not only upon subordinate animals such as the vanishing bison and the corresponding dodo, but also upon our own inferior human races.

For example, the Tasmanians, who in spite of their human physical likeness, were entirely swept out of existence in a war of extermination, a calamity that had been eagerly waged by antagonistic European immigrants. All of that carnage had occurred within the space of a mere half-century. Are we such apostles of phony mercy and fraudulent self-pity as to complain if the Martians warred in the same spirit as our own covetous, exploring Caucasian settlers?

The ambitious shit-head Martians seem to have calculated their race's prospective extinction with amazing subtlety, and their mathematical learning had evidently been far in excess of our deficient arithmetic, and the on-a-mission alien beings had been conniving to carry-out their detailed war preparations with perfect precision and with a unanimity of spirit.

Had our superficial telescopes allowed our brains to materialize advanced abstract thinking, we boneheads might have seen the gathering trouble far back in the early nineteenth century, and we could have better prepared for interplanetary battle.

Men like Schiaparelli had intensely watched the red planet, and it is wildly odd that for countless centuries, Mars has been the red star of war, named after the Roman deity of destructive combat. But that cataract-visioned fellow, Schiaparelli, devoid of a first name, failed to interpret the fluctuating appearances of the markings that he and his myopic-sighted colleagues had so erroneously mapped-out. All that totally futile and fruitless time, the surreptitious Martians must have been getting ready, willing, and able to initiate their fantastically mendacious strategy.

During the 1894 Martian scrutiny of Earth, a great light had been seen upon the illuminated part of the distant disk, first being viewed at the Lick Observatory, where the fake tabloids have falsely described the dedicated astronomers as being "pussy lappers". Then soon thereafter, the astronomical event had been documented by Perrotin of Nice, who like Schiaparelli, also never revealed his first name. And then days later, flares emanating from Mars had been detected by other pompous celestial observers.

Avid English readers had learned of those "meteors" first in the issue of *Nature,* dated August 2, 1894. I am inclined to think that those distinct red planet blazes may have been the blasting of huge cannons, in the vast pit sunk into *their* mostly desolate planet, from which their preliminary shots were rapidly fired toward us here in England. Peculiar geometric Martian markings, as yet unexplained, were noticeably seen near the site of that outbreak on Mars during the next two weeks of similar flashing activity.

The determined Martians were neither bozos nor buffoons. Their apparent principal objective was the conquest of the unwary Earth, the subjugation of our planet's remaining and surviving occupants, and the pernicious devastation of all former earthly culture and accompanying civilization.

The gathering storm burst upon us one year ago to this very calendar day. As Mars approached opposition, Lavelle of Java, who never slept because the dipshit incessantly drank coffee day and night, activated the telegraph wires of the astronomical exchange, and precisely recorded a huge outbreak of incandescent gas being emitted from the red planet.

The Martian's bold military maneuver had occurred towards midnight; and the spectroscope, to which Lavelle had at once resorted, exactly indicated a mass of flaming non-intestinal gas, chiefly hydrogen, moving with an enormous velocity towards this targeted Earth. This threatening jet of fire had dissipated and had become invisible about a quarter past twelve.

Ironically, Lavelle of Java, who like Schiaparelli and Perrotin, was devoid of a first name, compared the impressive explosion to a colossal "flame puff", which suddenly and violently squirted-out of the red planet, "comparable to flaming gases inexplicably rushing-out of a tobacco-less smoking gun."

Yet, the next day, because of a wildcat labor strike, there was an absence of reporting *that* particular astronomical phenomenon in the daily papers, except a minor note penned by a scab reporter in the *Daily Telegraph,* and consequently, the literate world went in ignorance of the gravest, most imminent danger that ever threatened the human race.

I might not have heard of the Martian eruption at all had I not met Ogilvy, the well-known, no-first-name, bald-headed, garrulous astronomer at Ottershaw, where all of the females were reputed to have hairy beavers. Ogilvy had been immensely excited at reading the downplayed, brief periodical news, and in the excess of his usually-suppressed feelings, that memorable night, the nutcase astronomer invited me up to his place of employment to alternately take turns with him, keenly engaging-in an analytical scrutiny of the red sphere.

In spite of all that has happened since *that* evening, I still remember that unique vigil very distinctly: the dark and silent observatory; the shadowed lantern throwing a feeble glow upon the floor over in the left corner; the steady ticking of the clockwork slow movement of the heavy telescope; and the narrow slit in the observatory's roof, which presented an oblong perception with the stardust sky canopy marvelously drifting across it.

Ogilvy deliberately-but-anxiously moved about the premises, scarcely visible, but his staccato, feminine-like voice being quite audible.

Looking through the telescope, my curious pupils noticed a circle of sinister-in-appearance, deep blue sparkles, and then finally, perceived the recognition of a little round red planet swimming in the vast, navy-blue background field. Mars seemed like such an innocent, harmless little object, so bright, small and still, faintly marked with various transverse stripes, presumably canals, and slightly flattened-in-stature from being perfectly round.

But so tiny in dimension was our new-found nemesis, so silvery warm in deceiving appearance, suggesting to my disheveled mind a pin's head of light! Mars seemed to be predictably quivering, but in reality, this personal observation was actually the telescope vibrating with the activity of the clockwork that kept the distant planet's gradual movement in discernible view.

As I watched the intriguing spectacle with fascination, the planet seemed to grow larger and smaller, and also, to peculiarly advance and recede, but *that* accounting was simply the fact that my restless right eye was rather tired. Forty million miles separated Mars from *us* had, at that point in time, indeed constituted forty million miles of absolute lifeless void. Few people realize the vacant immensity of the obscure emptiness in which the planets systematically swim.

I recall that in the background of Planet Mars, within the observable field, were three faint points of light, the isosceles triangle being formed by three telescopic stars infinitely remote, and all around the mysterious red planet was the enveloping darkness of vacuous space.

You might know from winter experience exactly how that aforementioned blackness looks on a frosty, starlit night. However, through a telescope's lens, visibility seems far more profound. And the overall visual perception was rather remarkable to me because Mars was so remote and so small, seemingly a miniscule micro-organism flying swiftly and steadily towards me, slowly moving across that incredible distance, drawing nearer every minute by so many thousands of miles.

My eyes were amazed by the "Thing" that the nefarious alien perpetrators were sending towards us; yes, it was the original lethal Thing that was to bring so much struggle, turmoil, calamity and death to the residents of Mother Earth, especially now dwelling in metropolitan London and vicinity. I never remotely dreamed of the prospective danger then, as I curiously watched the awesome detonations occurring. Obviously, no breathing numbskull on Planet Earth had ever dreamed about the lethal potential of those first several earthbound missiles.

That night, too, there was a third jetting-out of gas emanating from the distant planet's equator. I witnessed it heading in Earth's direction with incredulous eyes. A reddish flash flared-out at the edge, characterized by the slightest projection of the blast's azure-blue-green outline, just as the accurate chronometer struck midnight. And at that eerie interval, I told Ogilvy about the enigma, and the then-neurotic fellow enthusiastically took my place at the immense telescope.

The night was warm, my tongue was parched, and I was thirsty, so like a blind asshole, I clumsily departed the vicinity and awkwardly stretched my legs. I ineptly hobbled my way in the darkness, with my destination being the little table where the siphon stood, while Ogilvy astonishingly exclaimed several foul expletives about the extraordinary stream of gas that had been heading-out towards us.

That night, another Martian missile started on its trajectory toward the Earth, four hours after the first blue-green ray had originated. I remember how I sat upon the table like an immobile human vegetable, scared shitless in the obscure blackness, and without the aid of a telescope, having patches of green and crimson swirling and whirling before my eyes.

I wished that I had a light to smoke my short stogie, all-the-while, little suspecting the meaning of the tiny gleam which I had recently observed, and my addled mind failing to fathom all the unexpected information that the distant manifestation would surprisingly bring me. At that moment, I never even speculated that a clandestine Martian invasion had been initiated.

Old Fart Ogilvy watched the distant planet until one in the morning, and then gave-up his grueling pursuit. And next, the astronomer lit his reliable lantern, and soon we sauntered-over to his nearby hilltop house in the Red-Light District of town. Down below, outlined in the gloomy darkness, were Ottershaw and Chertsey, along with all their hundreds of lethargic and indolent residents, all sleeping in peace and notably unaware of any impending extraterrestrial threat.

Diarrhea-prone Ogilvy was full of speculation (and feces) that night, with his slurred, lisping words very apprehensively expressing bizarre language about the unbearable living conditions on Mars, and the gaseous jerk scoffed and farted at the vulgar idea of the red planet having intelligent, doomed inhabitants, who were fearfully attempting to signal their distress to us.

The astronomer's main idea conveyed to me was that meteorites might be turbulently falling in a heavy shower upon the planet, since Mars is separated from Jupiter by the notorious asteroid belt. And Ogilvy also mentioned that a huge volcano had possibly exploded upon Mars's surface, and the ongoing dilemma, being witnessed, was visually in progress here on Earth.

When my annoying acquaintance finally stopped passing gas, I fully comprehended that my illustrious companion was no longer farting around. The quixotic moron verbally pointed-out to me how unlikely it was that the same organic evolution had inadvertently taken the same maturing direction in the Solar System's two adjacent planets.

"The chances against anything human-like in nature being active on Mars are at least a million-to-one," Ogilvy uttered as if he was an ethnocentric Junior Nostradamus. "It just ain't in the cards," the fucked-up, superstitious astronomer vociferously added, as the adult ignoramus casually examined his favorite tarot deck spread-out upon his kitchen table.

Hundreds of alert observers around the world simultaneously saw the distant celestial flame that evening, and also, the following night immediately after midnight, and again the night thereafter. And so, for ten consecutive evenings, a familiar faint flare had been featured, being specifically generated toward Earth from Mars.

Why the brilliant shots ceased after the tenth magnificent demonstration, no qualified spectators on Earth had endeavored to explain. "It may be that the gases being fired had caused the Martians grave inconvenience," Ogilvy sophomorically stated while simultaneously farting a nasty volley of rather-noxious, intestinal odor that seemingly saturated the whole oxygen inside his utilitarian kitchen.

Dense clouds of smoke or dust, visible through a powerful telescope on Earth as little grey, fluctuating patches, spread through the clearness of the distant planet's atmosphere, and thoroughly obscured its more identifying features.

"The erratic Martians are evidently shooting green and brown bursts of fecal projectiles in our direction, so I've concluded that the audacious creatures are indeed full of shit!" exhausted Ogilvy un-sagely hypothesized and declared.

Even the drowsy and incompetent morning newspaper reporters finally woke-up to finally describe the unusual celestial disturbances, and popular back-page articles and news columns appeared here, there, and everywhere concerning the unpredictable volcanic activity occurring on Mars. The comical periodical *Punch,* "the hilarious sister-publication of *Judy"*, made a happy use of the Martian emissions unintentionally demolishing the red planet in the zany political cartoon of the most-popular morning tabloid.

And many unsuspecting citizens throughout London had evaluated and opined that *those* interesting signals that the Martians had fired at us were drawing earthward, rushing at a pace of many miles a second through the empty gulf of space, hour by hour, and day by day, approaching our whereabouts, nearer and nearer.

It seems to me now, almost admirably wonderful that, with swift fate hanging over *our* ultimate destiny, that resilient men could go about their petty business without neither worry nor concern. I remember how jubilant Markham, who also lacked a first name, was at securing a new photograph of the planet for the illustrated morning paper, which the neurotic imbecile irresponsibly and haphazardly had edited and magnified in those former ideal, calm days.

British people in those latter times scarcely realized the abundance of enterprise lacking in our nineteenth-century papers' mediocre narratives. For my own part, at the time, I was much-preoccupied in learning how to skillfully ride the new-fangled invention known as "the bicycle", and almost instantaneously, I found myself searching for specific knowledge about Mars while being diverted reading a series of tabloid-oriented headlines, whose stories were discussing the probable development of contemporary moral ideas and issues, as civilization idealistically had been progressing from the current toxic Industrial Age to the more-exciting Scientific Era.

One night the following week, the first exploratory foreign missile had been around 10,000,000 miles away. I ventured-out for a casual stroll with my big-breasted wife, who required three very tight bras to prevent her enormous nipples from touching her ankles.

The sky was starlit, with the Milky Way being rather prominent, and I explained to my disinterested spouse the various Signs of the Zodiac, and authoritatively pointed-out Mars, a bright dot of light creeping zenith-ward, where so many British telescopes were appropriately pointing.

It was a warm night, and my mind had been surreptitiously thinking-about getting laid, and how I should approach the delicate matter with mammoth-breasted, cavern-crotched Beatrice. Approaching our home, a party of excursionists from either Chertsey or Isleworth passed by us singing erotic sex songs, and the jovial revelers were producing silly tribal jungle music while pounding-upon improvised drums.

There were lights in the upper windows of the neighboring houses as the fatigued residents went to bed to engage in boring and monotonous humping and pumping. From the distant railway station came the sounds of arriving and departing trains, the huge locomotives ringing and rumbling, and eventually, the distracting noises eventually becoming softened. But still, the dissonant rhythms were sounding like a non-romantic, obnoxious melody fading in the distance.

My demonstrative wife pointed-out the brightness of the red, green, and yellow railroad signal lights hanging in a framework against the night sky. The entire tranquil environment seemed so safe and serene.

Then, giving my desire to have sex the green light, Beatrice stopped ambling and eagerly pointed to her crotch, and I quickly understood that my wife strongly desired to get laid, thus compatibly satisfying our dual mutual lusts.

'Screw the planet Mars and its highly peculiar flare activity,' I greedily thought. 'It's now time to lustfully screw Beatrice right through the damned bedroom mattress, before she begins reading her nightly porno' magazines!'

Chapter 2

"THE FALLING STAR"

Then, next came the ominous night featuring the first falling star. The streaking image was seen by a few local residents at dawn, zipping eastward, and rendering a line of flames high in the upper atmosphere. The local cottage dwellers had taken the stratospheric sensation to be just an ordinary falling star, and did not describe the event as being any great marvel.

Albin, a bleach-skinned albino, and also a wholly gay, one-name biologist, described the fantastic sky-line as leaving a greenish tinge behind, which brightly glowed for several seconds. Denning, our greatest one-name local authority on meteorites, stated that the height of the meteor's first appearance was about ninety to one hundred miles above terra-firma. It seemed to Denning that the meteor had fallen to Earth around twenty-miles east of his specific location at the time.

I was at home at *that* particular early twilight hour, performing research and writing a scientific journal article inside my private study. And although my French windows face towards Ottershaw, and the blinds were up (for I loved in those days to glance at the night sky), I saw nothing of the dawn spectacle, for being an addicted voyeur, I had been euphorically searching for a certain town doll's young brown beaver, usually being exposed in her upstairs open-shade window.

Yet, this strangest of all things that ever descended to Earth from outer space must have fallen while I had been sitting there in my study, had I only looked-up from my vicarious porno' preoccupation when the Object had swiftly passed overhead. Some of those startled citizens in nearby communities who had observed its flight stated that it traveled with a weird hissing noise. I myself heard nothing of that sort, not even from my twelve snakes, soundly sleeping in my secured glass aquarium.

Many people in Berkshire, in Surrey, and also those third-gender-transvestites living in Middlesex, must have also perceived the wondrous phenomenon, and at most, must have thought that just another wandering meteor had sped by. No one in Maybury Hill seemed to have troubled looking for the fallen mass later that morning.

But very early, Ogilvy, who had astutely seen the "shooting star", and who was persuaded that a meteorite had landed somewhere on the common between Horsell, Ottershaw, and Woking, decided early to go exploring the vicinity and finding it. Locate it he did, and not far from the shallow, all-too-familiar quarry sand-pits.

An enormous crater had been formed by the direct impact of the outer-space projectile, and the soft sand and gravel had been flung violently in every direction over the heath, forming immense mounds that were lucidly visible a mile away. The heather had soon set on fire eastward, and a thin blue smoke rose against the early dawn's illumination.

The Thing itself lay almost entirely buried in sand, resting amidst the scattered splinters of a dozen or so fir trees, which *it* had disintegrated into large, toothpick-like fragments during its tremendous horizontal impact. The exposed part of the Object displayed the appearance of being a huge cylinder, thinly caked-over with silt, and its outline softened by a thick, scaly incrustation. The assumed "Meteorite" had a sizable diameter of about thirty yards.

Ogilvy cautiously approached the smoky mass, and was surprised at its general circumference, but more so stunned at the item's irregular shape, since most meteorites are basically rounded in form, more or less.

The steaming Thing was, however, still so hot from its flight through the atmosphere as to temporarily limit the captivated investigator's careful approach.

A stirring noise originating from within the cylinder intrigued Ogilvy, the itinerant astronomer, who later ascribed the hissing to the unequal cooling of its apparent metallic surface; for at that time, the notion had not yet occurred to the newly-arrived inspector that the interior of the crashed Thing might indeed be hollow.

Astounded, Ogilvy remained standing stationary at the edge of the blazing pit that the Thing had excavated for itself, peering-down in amazement at its symmetrical-but-strange appearance, but also being rather emotionally astonished, chiefly at the half-sunken Object's unusual composition and pulsating color. And even then, the shocked discoverer had been dimly viewing tangible evidence of "intelligent design" that was quite evident upon "the mechanism's" spectacular arrival.

The early morning had been wonderfully still, and the rising sun, just clearing the pine trees towards somnolent Weybridge, was already somewhat warm. Ogilvy did not remember hearing any birds chirping or squawking that significant spring morning, and according to his later testimony, there was certainly no frigid breeze stirring, and the only detectable sounds were the faint movements coming from within the cryptic cylinder. The bewildered astronomer was all alone upon the common, and had no one with whom to share his drastic predicament.

Then suddenly, the petrified scientist noticed with a start that some of the grey debris, the ashy incrustation that covered the supposed meteorite, was gradually falling-off the circular edge near its ends. The external remnants were slowly rotating, the revolutions dropping-off huge dislodged flakes, which were raining-down upon the already-disturbed nearby sand. A large piece suddenly came-off and fell with a distinct noise that brought Ogilvy's vibrating heart almost up into his wide-open mouth.

"What the fuck is this shit?" my mind now recollects the then-petrified astronomer later informing me. "I have no more wet or solid crap to excrete out of my delicate asshole!"

For a minute, the early morning adventurer scarcely realized exactly what *that* sinister "other-world activity" truly meant, and although the surrounding heat had been excessive, Ogilvy gathered sufficient courage to intrepidly clamber-down into the smoke-laden cavity, and the investigator adroitly arrived close to the Object's bulk in order to assess "the Thing" more clearly.

The porno' enthusiast, who belonged to Beatrice's Porn Recitation Club, fancied that the slow-cooling of the "device" might account for the peculiar oozing-steam sound, but what disturbed *that* idea was the fact that the floating ashes were falling only from the sealed ends of the huge cylinder. 'I wonder if any Martian whores or hookers are stashed inside!' the totally psychotic, weirdo pervert creatively speculated. 'If so, I might need to obtain some Martian money in a hurry!'

And then, the telescope expert employed at the observatory frightfully comprehended that the partially-exposed cylinder's circular top was slowly rotating on its shaft. 'Damn it! I want to get laid, but this alien Thing is doing the real screwing!' Ogilvy regrettably conjectured.

According to the anxious observer, the cap was engaged in such a dynamic, silent movement that my star-gazing friend had discovered it by only noticing that a black shadow, which had been near him five minutes before, had then appeared at the opposite side of the Object's jagged apex. Even then, my demented acquaintance scarcely fathomed exactly what that complicated other-world furtive operation dramatically indicated, until Ogilvy soon heard a perceptible, muffled, grating sound, and his alarmed pupils instantly noticed that the black mark had jerked forward an inch or so.

Then, a true and valid hypothesis came upon him in a wonderful flash. The assumed meteor was indeed artificial and hollow, with an entrance and exit end that mechanically screwed-out! But something or someone within the cylinder had been unscrewing the lid!

"Good heavens!" Ogilvy loudly exclaimed to no-one in his company. "There's possibly a spaceman inside; or perhaps little green men from the red planet! Maybe they're now half-broiled to death; their tender nuts roasting like chestnuts over an open Christmas fire! I think they're possibly trapped inside, trying to escape their excruciating hell!"

At once, with a quick and erudite mental leap, Ogilvy instantly became magnificently sagacious, and the excited astronomer's debilitated brain linked the half-buried Thing with the recent flashes occurring on Mars.

The thought of the confined creature (or creatures) was so dreadful to the naïve scientist that the confused fellow forgot about the intense heat, and his corpulent body soon clambered forward toward the sunken cylinder to help loosen the hatch.

But luckily, the dull radiation being generated arrested Ogilvy's forward progress before the daring fool could egregiously burn his bare hands upon the still-glowing metallic lid. At that interval, the befuddled asshole stood irresolute for a moment; then he turned, scrambled-out of the fuming pit, and cravenly dashed-off, running wildly into neighboring Woking, where no one had yet awoken.

The approximate time must have been somewhere before six a.m. The flustered sprinter soon met a wagoner and tried to make the illiterate garbage collector understand the prospect of "the alien machine down in the crater", but the tale that my acquaintance wildly disclosed, along with his soiled appearance, together seemed so implausible and unbelievable. The fully crazed fanatic divulged to the donkey-cart driver that *his* cherished fedora had fallen off into the recently-dug pit, and the amused cart driver simply whipped his mule and drove ahead to collect more rubbish.

"Stop talking trash!" the perturbed junk gatherer protested and yelled. "And I absolutely know fake word-salad garbage when I hear it. And I also know a fucked-up cretin such as yourself as soon as I see and hear his first exclamatory sentence!"

Ogilvy was equally unsuccessful with the early-morning potman, who had been busy unlocking the doors of the public-shithouse, situated next to pungent-smelling Horsell Bridge. The industrious fellow thought that the shouting solicitor was a full-fledged lunatic at large, and aggressively made an unsuccessful attempt at shoving and shutting the hysterical messenger inside the public crap-house.

That violent incident sobered-up the amateur Hermes a little, and when Ogilvy spotted Henderson, a one-name self-conscious London journalist taking a lengthy piss inside *his* weed-infested garden, the delirious courier called over the stone wall and curtly made himself noticed.

"Henderson," the nervous star-gazer beckoned. "Did you see that glorious shooting star early this morning?"

"Well?" answered Henderson. "The shooting star with the gigantic machine gun! Ha, ha, ha!"

"It's crashed out on Horsell Common, right now."

"Good Lord!" Henderson loudly exclaimed. "Fallen meteorite! That's good. Maybe later today I can go visit over there and chip-off some unknown interstellar minerals with my trusty hammer and chisel!"

"But it's something more than a regular, ordinary meteorite," Ogilvy excitedly replied to the penny-pinching chiseler. "It's a fuckin' cleverly-constructed cylinder; a gigantic artificial, metallic cylinder, I say! And there's something or someone trapped inside."

Henderson stood-up with his spade in his hand, quite anxious to learn more particulars.

"What's that?" the acclaimed award-winning gardener replied. "I'm completely deaf in one ear. Do you think it's a futuristic robot trapped inside? Maybe dear Ogilvy, the off-course space alien navigator has three huge dicks along with seven diminutive testicles! Ha, ha, ha!"

Ogilvy next told Henderson all that he had seen and heard at the newly-formed pit. The humored listener required a minute or so to accurately file the orated summary inside his suspicious thought processes. Then, feeling rejuvenated, the audience-of-one dropped his spade, snatched-up his jacket, and eagerly paced-out onto the cobblestone road.

The two allied men hurried at once to the common, and just outside the rural park setting, the twosome immediately found the metallic cylinder still lying in the same position as when Ogilvy had first discovered it.

But now, the former uncanny sounds inside had ceased, and a thin circle of bright metal presently showed between the queer cylinder's top and its interior body. Air was either entering or escaping at the rim with a thin, sizzling sound, which suggested to the pair of educated observers that an actual living creature had somehow miraculously survived the terrific ground impact.

The mesmerized men intently listened, rapped upon the scaly, burnt metal with an available tree branch, and then, meeting with no palpable response, the exhilarated duo prematurely concluded that the man, men, or unfortunate extraterrestrials stuck inside must be severely injured, or perhaps even dead.

Of course, the now-exhausted local trekkers were quite unable to do anything essential in the line of rescue. The outsiders shouted a flurry of consolations and promises, and feeling frightened, instantly darted-off back to town in order to obtain additional help.

"That cylinder is not man-made," Henderson declared to Ogilvy as the pair sprinted ahead.

"Yes, you're right, Henderson! The fuckin' thing is out of this world!" frantically panted-back the astounded astronomer.

One can imagine the two very scared mortals, covered with sand and grit, neurotic and disordered, running like incensed maniacs up the main street in the bright sunlight, just as the shop proprietors were habitually taking-down their shutters, and people, needing a quantity of fresh air after getting laid, were strenuously opening their bedroom windows. Henderson at once meandered into the town railway station, for the purpose of telegraphing the sensational news to the major London newspapers, hoping to receive syndicated coverage of his eyewitness report.

Over the course of the week, various brief newspaper articles satirically prepared local residents' minds to be receptive of the joking idea of little green Martian visitors energetically dancing about, all seemingly masquerading and behaving like dumb-ass St. Patrick Day leprechauns.

By eight o'clock on that memorable morning, a number of boys and men had started-off toward the common to find evidence of the "dead men from Mars".

I myself had heard of Ogilvy and Henderson's descriptive account, receiving *their* misadventure first from my newspaper delivery boy at about a quarter to nine, when I had casually stepped-out my front door to retrieve my *Daily Chronicle*.

I was naturally quite startled upon hearing the eccentric report, and my curious mind, along with my physical being wasted little time in going-outside and ambling across the Ottershaw Bridge in the direction of the aforementioned "new landmark sand and gravel pits", and not knowing exactly what to expect.

Chapter 3

"HORSELL COMMON"

I soon found a small crowd of perhaps twenty gabbing people surrounding the huge hole into which the odd cylinder lay. I have already described the general appearance of that colossal hulk, presently half-embedded deeply into the ground. The turf and gravel scattered about the indecipherable Object had seemed charred, as if recently scorched by a sudden explosion. No doubt "the Machine's" forceful impact had caused a flash fire in the vicinity, and perhaps inside the metallic capsule itself.

I quickly ascertained that Henderson and Ogilvy were not presently integrated amongst the assembled bystanders. I think the two scurrilous assholes were still unnerved by their dramatic encounter, and the dimwits decided that currently, nothing was to be done in terms of extensive excavation. So, the lethargic pair, I presumed, had sanctimoniously gone away to breakfast at Henderson's gaudy house across the common.

There were four or five punk boys sitting upon the jagged edge of the pit, with their feet and weatherworn shoes dangling, merrily amusing themselves until I daringly commenced throwing stones at the partially hidden giant mass. After I had lectured to the young delinquents about their public deportment becoming more careful and discreet, the juvenile nutcases began playing a frivolous game of "touch my crotch", insolently scurrying in and out of gathered groups of chatting spectators.

Among those adulterous adults were a couple of bicyclists; a drunken gardener; several marijuana dealers; a pregnant teenage girl already carrying a baby; Gregg the village butcher, accompanied by his tiny transgender boy, along with two or three helmeted loafers and midget golf caddies from Leatherhead, who were accustomed and enamored to habitually hanging-about the dusty and ramshackle Woking Railway Station.

In those nostalgic olden days, when academic education was considered not a major priority, few of the British common people possessed anything but the vaguest mastery of modern astronomical concepts. Most of the dumbfounded assholes were at the time of my arrival staring quietly at the big, exposed section of the massive cylinder, which was still intact, exactly as Ogilvy and Henderson had left it.

I imagined that the popular expectation of removing charred alien corpses from the internal compartment was being conversed by the local authorities, while the crowd was preoccupied simply gazing and peering at that inanimate bulk. Some bored individuals went away from the scene while I was there, and other curious morons coincidentally arrived and took *their* places.

I valiantly-but-deliberately clambered-down into the hollow and fancied I heard a faint movement originating from within the metallic sphere. Hearing several gasps from female onlookers standing above, my sensitive ears also discerned a disconcerting, low, auditory vibration being emitted from within the metallic capsule. I felt a sort of surreal solace in recognizing that the Object's top had certainly ceased its methodical rotation.

It was only when I advanced relatively close to the unusual embedded 'Craft' that the basic strangeness of that inexplicable 'Mechanism' became evident to my rattled instincts. At the first impressionable glance, the ULO (Unidentified Landed Object) was then really no more exciting than an overturned carriage, or perhaps as interesting as an ordinary, uprooted tree that had been fiercely blown across the road after a violent tornado. In truth, to my eyes, it looked something like a rusty, traveling carnival or common county fair amusement carriage, pushed deeply into the ground.

'Brownish rust is iron oxide,' I rationally discerned, 'and the grey outer scale of this eccentric Thing is analogous to no common patina, or known chemical oxide. That peculiar yellowish-white metal, gleaming in the visible crack between the lid and the cylinder, engenders an unfamiliar, foreign hue.'

The science-fiction terminology *extra-terrestrial* had no special meaning for most of the uneducated onlookers, many of whom never heard of prestigious scholarly institutions such as Eton and Cambridge. 'In fact, any of these imbeciles probably think that Oxford is a factory on the other side of London that manufactures a certain style of exquisite foot gear!' my perverted sense of humor reckoned.

At that convoluted time, it was quite clear in my own mind that "the Thing" had initiated its space journey from the planet Mars, but in my haste, I confidently endorsed the bizarre theory that the "Spaceship" probably *didn't* contain any living creature or navigating beings. I thought the unscrewing might actually be some programmed automatic procedure, or conversely, some unique, functioning robotic activity.

In spite of Ogilvy's dumb-ass dubious thinking, I still believed in the back of my mind that there were numerous "little green men" living on Mars. My distraught brain ran fancifully on the possibility that the metallic sphere had contained special salient manuscripts written in some kind of complicated hieroglyphics to challenge academic translation at various London universities. My wild imagination also conjectured that perhaps a highly qualified, competent salvage team would discover a trove of oddly minted coins inside, and so forth. Yet, the crashed vehicle was a little too large in size for confirmation of any of those fleeting, random 'science fiction-type-speculations'.

I recall feeling an annoying impatience at *not* seeing the lid becoming fully unscrewed and lifting open. About eleven that morning, being disappointed that nothing else of major consequence seemed to be happening, I decided not to return to my humble home over in Maybury Hill. But still being mentally distracted, I determined that it would be rather difficult for me to be sitting in my safe and secure study, endeavoring to diligently work upon my normal, abstract, research investigations, while all of this fascinating mayhem had been happening at the cryptic pit.

In the late afternoon, the appearance of the lazy towns' common grassy space had altered very much. The early editions of the evening newspapers had startled and alarmed the easily influenced London citizenry with enormous and exaggerated headlines:

"A MESSAGE RECEIVED FROM MARS." ## "REMARKABLE STORY FROM WOKING"

In addition, Ogilvy had dispatched a fucked-up wire to the Astronomical Exchange, which had automatically roused the attention of every corresponding observatory situated in the three separate kingdoms.

There were half-a-dozen ambulances, three fire wagons, and fifty human hearse chasers that had arrived from the chaotic Woking Train Station, standing in the road by the sand-pits, milling around a delivery wagon from Chobham, and admiring a rather lordly and ostentatious horse-drawn carriage. Ironically, many of the passenger train newcomers seemed to possess their own *loco-motives* for being there.

Besides the fairly-mundane, small-town scenario, there was quite a number of stationary bicycles parked in irregular rows, with their lackadaisical riders standing around, engaging in lackluster conversations.

In spite of the day's exceptional heat, a large array of people must have trekked from Woking and Chertsey, so that there was, altogether, quite a considerable crowd gathered, and also in attendance were several gaily-dressed, popular local prostitutes searching for mustached politicians, and also actively soliciting wealthy aristocrats wearing silk top-hats present within the throng.

Needless to report, near noontime, it was glaringly hot, with not a grey cloud in the sky nor a breath of soothing wind, and the only welcomed shadows were being cast from a few scattered pine trees. The burning heather had been effectively extinguished, but the level ground extending towards distant Ottershaw had been blackened from the conflagration as far as one could see, and the blaze's remnants were still giving-off occasional vertical smoke streams.

An enterprising sweet-stuff dealer in the Chobham Road had sent up his son with a barrow-load of green apples, ginger beer, candy, tampons, sex energy pills, and dildos to sell amongst the assembled stupid-shit, commonplace bystanders, who in reality, were mostly unemployed and had nothing better to do.

Advancing to the edge of the pit, I found that the hollow was currently being occupied by a group of about a half-dozen men, including Henderson, Ogilvy, and also a tall, fair-haired, venerable gentleman that I afterwards learned was named Stent, from the eminent Astronomer Royal, who was suffering (according to gossip) from a major heart and vascular malady.

In addition, several non-union workmen, who were wielding spades and pickaxes, had joined the impromptu conference transpiring inside and around the breach. Stent was imperatively giving directions in a clear, high-pitched voice, as if the arrogant fuck was the master-of-ceremonies at the infamous Woking LBGTQRSTUVW Bordello and Bistro.

That egotistical jerk-off Stent was seen standing on top of the 'other-world cylinder', which was now evidently somewhat cooler in temperature than an expired cigarette match. Stent's face was crimson and streaming with perspiration, and something seemed to have irritated him when the egocentric dipshit boisterously announced to the gathered laborers, "Okay, men. Don't sweat the small stuff! Let's get the fuck busy!"

Minutes later, a large portion of the entrenched cylinder had been skillfully uncovered, though its mysterious midsection and lower end were still deeply embedded underneath. As soon as Ogilvy noticed my presence among the highly-focused, staring crowd, the boisterous faggot bellowed for me to come-down to his position inside the hollow. The doltish dunce then asked if I would mind going over to confer a certain matter with Lord Hilton, the wealthy owner of the nearby manor house.

"The growing crowd," Stent revealed, "is quite obnoxious, and the nincompoops are becoming a serious impediment to our important excavations."

"Can't we just give them all a few pounds to buy some fabulous porno' magazines?" I creatively countered. "I'd wager that each of the undisciplined, hormone-driven scamps has yet to experience his first erection, let alone the thrill of his initial ejaculation!"

Showing defiance to adult authority, several of the junior dick-pullers wanted to jump over a flimsy railing that was being hastily put-up, in order to prevent the rambunctious juvenile derelicts from leaping directly into the pit. Stent austerely insisted and maintained to me that I should "supervise and control the acne-faced dipshits". But then the paranoid asshole firmly informed me, "A faint stirring is still occasionally audible within the 'Metallic Meteorite', but the team of muscular workmen, toiling assiduously with their shovels, has failed to completely dislodge the heavy top."

"Look Stent! Get the glamorous prostitutes standing over there to assist you in your fruitless endeavor," I argued, just to break the asshole's balls. "The talented whores know all about screwing, and perhaps, the sultry bitches are also professional authorities on unscrewing!" I intentionally joked, much to Stent's chagrin.

"The casement appears to be enormously thick, and it is logically possible that the faint sounds we had heard represented a last frantic effort to escape captivity and death inside the interior," Stent indignantly replied, ignoring my weak attempt at establishing a degree of humor, and maintaining a comedic dialogue.

Being intimidated, I was very glad to do as the infuriated hypocrite had asked, and so I voluntarily became one of the privileged spectators standing erect within the confines of the makeshift fenced-in enclosure, ineffectively reprimanding the horde of restive juvenile delinquents running in circles trying to pull one another's knickers down.

Several minutes later, becoming positively bored, I failed to locate mannerly Lord Hilton at his resplendent manor house, but I was told by a servant that the pompous scumbag was expected to arrive from London by the six o'clock train from Waterloo, 'unaccompanied by the egomaniac dictator, Napoleon'!"

And as it was then about a quarter past five on my fob chain watch, and having no desire to further participate in deplorable Stent's abominable clown-show, my mind conducted my abused feet to quietly amble back home to peaceful Maybury Hill.

By eight o'clock on that following morning, a number of curious boys and unemployed men had already started-off toward the common to find evidence of the "dead men from Mars".

I myself had heard of Ogilvy and Henderson's descriptive account, receiving *their* misadventure first hand after I had casually stepped-out my front door to retrieve my *Daily Chronicle,* and then conversing with a local store's errand runner.

I was naturally quite startled upon hearing the eccentric report, and my anxious mind, along with my physical being, wasted little time in ambling across the Ottershaw Bridge in the direction of the aforementioned landmark sand and gravel pits.

Chapter 4

"THE CYLINDER OPENS"

When I impatiently had left Beatrice to her domestic chores, I returned to the vicinity of the formerly picturesque country common. Scattered groups were hurrying from the direction of Woking, and four of the new arrivals were expeditiously hustling toward the Martian hollow. The rowdy crowd of two hundred or so folks was self-arranged in a circular formation around the open pit, and their outline from afar stood-out as appearing black against the lemon-yellow sky.

There were raised voices, and I was aware of some sort of visceral struggle that appeared to be occurring. Strange imaginings of wicked, reprehensible, little green men causing unprecedented human havoc passed through my puzzled mind. As I drew nearer to the source of the verbal clamor, I heard Stent's screechy voice loudly commanding:

"Keep back! Keep back!" the psychopath screamed. "Stay your distance!" the detestable weirdo exclaimed.

A pimple-faced boy came running towards me and fearfully hollered, "It's a-movin'! I say it's a movin'!" the junior jerk-off frantically reiterated. "It's a-screwin' and a-screwin' the lid out of the meteorite. I don't like it one iota. I'm a-gonna' scoot straight home to my homo' parents; yes, I am."

I lumbered onward to join the rather restive and talkative crowd, that was elbowing, bumping, and jostling one another, and the three opinionated lady prostitutes in attendance were being, by no means, the least physical.

"He's fallen into the pit!" cried a concerned laborer. "Stent's brief stint on this ass-backwards planet might now be over!"

"Keep back!" boomed several concerned workmen, defensively raising their heavy shovels. "Keep back!"

The crowd swayed back and forth with each member trying to obtain a more advantageous view of the dreary hollow, and I gingerly elbowed my way through the boisterous horde. Everyone seemed greatly excited while aggressively pushing and shoving. Then suddenly, my perceptive ears heard a peculiar humming originating from the unnatural pit.

"I say!" yelled Ogilvy. "Someone strong please help me keep these belligerent idiots from coming down here into this pit. We don't know what's making that aggravating noise from inside the confounded Thing, you know! Is it animals, vegetable or possibly mineral?"

I saw a handsome young man, a gay shop assistant from Woking, I believe, boldly standing upon the cylinder's lid and using his hands, desperately trying to scramble-out of the hole into which the unruly and crazed throng had pushed him.

"We all came from a hole at birth, and we all will return to a hole after we die!" some self-appointed, deranged parson screamed. "Wholly hole shit! Repent! The end is near!"

The opposite points of the cylinder's top rotated, which was being systematically screwed-out from within. Nearly two feet of shining screw projected above the mechanism's arcane lid. Somebody behind my standing position awkwardly blundered against me, and I narrowly missed being pitched onto the top of the still slowly rotating screw, now quite elevated a half-foot above the cylinder's entrance hatch.

I turned, and as I did so, the huge, threaded screw must have come out completely, for the cylinder's cap fell upon the pit's gravel wall, with a strange-sounding ringing concussion. I accidentally stuck my bony elbow into the ribs of the unfortunate person pushing behind me, and instinctively, I again turned my head towards the eerie Thing. For a pregnant moment, that circular cavity below seemed perfectly black inside. I had the sunset rays affecting my eyes, and my visual perception had been negatively stifled.

I think everyone at the common expected to see a futuristic little green man emerge from the aperture, possibly something somewhat in appearance like us terrestrial males, but in all essential features, still a recognizable man. At the time, I too anticipated seeing a triumphant tiny humanoid emerging through the metal portal.

But, looking inside the opaque darkness more acutely, my eyes noticed something peculiar stirring within the shadow: the image was slightly greyish, showing billowy movements, one tentacle swaying above another, and then freakishly, two luminous disk-like eyes quickly appeared peering upwards.

Next, something wriggling, resembling a little grey snake, about the thickness of a walking stick in size, coiled-up out of its writhing midriff, and wiggled in the air towards my quivering hand, with a second moving tentacle soon becoming distinctly visible.

A sudden chill enveloped my terrified spirit. There was a loud shriek from a woman's throat before she fainted and collapsed upon the sandy turf. I half-turned, keeping my eyes fixed upon the now-diabolical cylinder, from which other sinister tentacles were soon projecting, and I began vigorously pushing my way back through the hysterical mob, hastily retreating from the pit's edge. My pupils objectively witnessed mortal astonishment giving place to intensified horror, all being exhibited upon the faces of the skittish humans that were wildly panicking in my midst.

My ears heard inarticulate exclamations permeating on all sides of my physical environment. There was a general unanimous movement thrusting backwards, away from the seemingly hostile cylinder's exit.

My eyes noticed the normally-placid shopman vehemently shouting and struggling, still tottering to-and-fro while attempting to successfully keep his jeopardized balance upon the detached lid's surface. Looking around, I suddenly found myself being alone, and my brain instantly fathomed the agitated people, who had been formerly jostling with others around the hole's circumference, scampering off to safety, with craven Stent evacuating among the human stampede.

I again glimpsed at the awesome foreign 'Spacecraft', and a heightened degree of ungovernable terror gripped my soul. I stood petrified in a fully mesmerized state, chronically staring below as if hypnotized.

A stupendous rounded bulk, perhaps the size of a ferocious grizzly bear, was rising slowly and apparently painfully, out of the cylinder's dark interior. As the creature (or Thing) bulged-up and caught the light, its formidable, disgusting, bleak-in-appearance, malignant-looking skin wondrously glistened like wet fish scales.

Two large, dark-colored eyes were scrupulously regarding me with steadfast concentration. The wrinkled mass that framed them, that is, the oval head of the Thing, was rounded in dimension, and possessed a horrendous-looking, snake-like countenance.

There was a fucked-up mouth positioned under the creepy grey eyes, featuring the lipless brim of a toothless maw, which intermittently quivered and panted, and soon thereafter, its lips crudely dropping or oozing putrid saliva strands from its distorted-looking maw.

The whole 'serpent' heaved and pulsated convulsively, just like a displaced, extra-terrestrial jellyfish. A lank tentacular appendage extended-out toward my right leg, which I assumed was a human hand substitute, and the revolting organ tightly gripped the cylinder's edge, while another "feeler" frenetically swayed in the air.

'This is some sort of intelligent Martian octopus that must have piloted this meteor through space!' I remember imagining. 'The creature looks like it could easily strangle a frenzied adult hippopotamus!'

Those who have never seen the behavior of a living Martian can scarcely comprehend the strange horror of its grotesque appearance. The peculiar V-shaped mouth with its pointed upper lip; the absence of brow ridges; the presence of a grotesque chin beneath the wedge-like lower lip; the incessant vibrating of that nauseating mouth; the absence of large nostrils; the reprehensible Gorgon, snake-like tentacles; the tumultuous deep breathing of alien lungs inhaling a strange atmosphere's oxygen; the evident heaviness and painfulness of physical movement due to the greater gravitational pull of the

Earth, and above all else, the hideous, immense, insect-like eyes, altogether, had made my empty stomach want to reactively vomit.

The repulsive-looking navigator inside the space cylinder had similar facial features to humans that evidently, had undergone a separate evolutionary pattern of development on the red planet. The repugnant grey facial features were most pathetic, nauseating, and monstrous, being especially reprehensible to my sense of human normality. My initial assessment was that the Martian pilot seemed a refugee from our own planet's prehistoric times.

There was something about the reptilian skin that suggested fungus pigmentation in the oily, grey/brown epidermis; yes, something morbid being depicted in the clumsy, deliberate, tedious movements that truly demonstrated a nasty, worm-like existence. Even at that initial direct confrontation, during my first abbreviated glimpse, I had naturally become overwhelmed with both horror and dread.

Suddenly, the ugly monster vanished into the depth of the chamber below. It had successfully toppled-over the cylinder's lid, and perhaps being injured or exhausted, had plummeted or vanished from the brim into the machine's interior, and with an abrupt thud, the Martian's landing sounded like the fall of a great mass of leather over in Leatherhead.

I heard the space alien give-out a peculiar, dense squeal, and forthwith, another of those abhorrent creatures appeared below, apparently to administer medical assistance, moving like a grey specter in the deep shadow of the semi-exposed aperture.

Feeling quite appalled, I hurriedly turned and, dashing madly, made my swift departure for the first clump of trees, situated perhaps a hundred-yards away. But I steadfastly bustled forward, slantingly, and stumbling along my escape, my body ultimately falling to the ground, and then, my left cheek scraping against a rock.

There, among some young pine trees and assorted yew bushes, I had stopped my running and panting, and feeling momentarily safe lying and bleeding there, my heart solemnly waited to interpret further abnormal developments.

Several minutes later, I slowly rose and walked the common, part of it now-circling around the once familiar natural sand dunes; around the stretch of trees; around grass and heather that was dotted with volatile, baffled people, most of whom were standing around like animated statues. The verbose gossipers, with their compelling narratives, their words being half-fascinated with recently viewed reality, and those same separate raucous-but-mediocre emotional conversations, also being motivated by very justified terror.

"What the fuck was inside that atrocious Thing?" an upset woman asked her stupefied male companion. "That grey creature looked a little bit like the fabled Medusa!"

"I think the ugly animal inside was a renegade reptile from Mars!" her flustered companion expressed. "Yes; the Thing was not of this world!"

"That's all the fuck we need!" the delirious woman ranted and shrieked. "We already have too many fucked-up, scaly-skinned, slimy lizards slithering-around this imperfect Earth! I say, see ya' later alligator! Let's get the hell out of here!"

And then, with a renewed horror, I keenly observed a round, black object bobbing up and down upon the edge of the deep pit. It was the head of the muscular shopman who had inadvertently fallen inside the hole. At first, I had thought that the fellow had been decapitated, but then, I fathomed that the maniacal shopman had managed to get his shoulder and knee up above the cylinder's ledge, and again the determined fellow seemed to slip back until only his whole head was visible.

Suddenly, the shopman's body totally vanished, and my ears detected a faint shriek of distress emitted from his strained vocal cords. I had a momentary impulse to heroically leap inside the space capsule and render help, but my accumulated fear prevailed, dominating and overruling my sense of humanity.

Everything below and inside the metallic cylinder was then quite obscure, especially hidden by the deep pit's shadows, along with the shadows caused from the high heap of surrounding sand that the cylinder's forceful impact had produced.

Anyone coming along the road from either Chobham or Woking would have surely been amazed at the outlandish sight inside the newly-formed sand and gravel pit, with a dwindling multitude of perhaps a hundred brave souls still loudly conversing while standing in distant narrow ditches.

Many of the chatterers were also sporadically stationed behind bushes, gates, fences, and hedges, the incredulous individuals uttering excited words to one another, with the common phrase of verbal exchange among the remaining stragglers being the interrogative, "What the fuck just happened?"

An hour later, the singular ginger beer and chocolate candy "barrow boy" still stood upon the almost-deserted common, and stuck in the nearby sand-pits was a row of abandoned horse-drawn vehicles, with their stallions either feeding out of attached nosebags, or their hoofs actively pawing the sterile ground.

Chapter 5

"THE HEAT RAY"

After the unforgettable glimpse I had had of the unworldly Martians, vaguely emerging from their enigmatic cylinder, inside which the lizard-like maniacs had surreptitiously occupied the interior, a kind of ethereal fascination paralyzed my bodily actions. I remained standing ankle-deep in the dense heather, staring at the far-away sand mound that had partially hidden the scumbags' mysterious machine. The yellow sand mass looked as if it truly belonged somewhere in the Sahara. In short, my mental quandary was a foggy battleground of combined emotional fear struggling-against and combating mental curiosity.

I did not dare venture back towards the ominous pit, but my ego felt a passionate inclination to once again arrive and peer-down into it. I began hastily walking, therefore, in a rather altered curve, seeking some safe vantage-point to conduct my intended investigation from a distance, and my wary pupils were continually gazing at the sand-piles that concealed those hideous-looking 'other-world invaders'.

As I stood gazing from behind a thick oak, my bloodshot eyes perceived a leash of thin blackish/grey whips, maneuvering about the Martian aperture, like the arms of a neurotic octopus. And a half-minute later, the visual manifestation ceased when the writhing tentacles were immediately withdrawn down inside the cylinder.

And soon afterwards, a narrow metallic rod rose-up, joint-by-joint, bearing at its apex a circular disk that wildly rotated like a spinning toy top, exhibiting an unorthodox wobbling motion.

'What kind of Martian bullshit could be going on there?' I skeptically wondered. 'These red planet piss-heads are giving my troubled brain a very serious cerebral meltdown!'

Most of the appalled country spectators had gathered into two separate remote groups; one being a little crowd over towards Woking, and the other constituting a knot of people in the direction of Chobham.

'Evidently, the local residents all share the same disturbing mental and emotional conflict as myself,' I tensely reasoned. 'Curiosity killed the cat!' my mind metaphorically recalled.

One elderly codger I had approached, I recollect, was an intimidated village neighbor of mine, but at first, neither of us had the social wherewithal to even begin articulating a standard conversation.

"What ugly *brutes!*" Frank Johnson disgustedly indicated. "Good God, Wells! What demonic, ugly brutes! Their fucked-up mothers must be whoring sea serpents!" my fellow Maybury Hill neighbor repeated over and over again.

"Did you see a man maneuvering inside the pit?" I nervously asked Johnson. "I believe the creature I had witnessed was a contemptible Martian visitor to Earth! But I'll tell you, Johnson!" I firmly communicated. "I know as you do that a Martian is not a little green-skinned asshole, and who probably does not have green blood flowing through his or her arteries and veins! And one more thing, Frank! I wonder what the hell a Martian's Johnson looks like!"

But in response to my comment, Frank Johnson only began checking his crotch area for urine stains, and the old goat failed to utter a viable reply to my relevant statement. We both then became silent, and stood side-by-side behind the wide oak, each of us deriving a certain comfort and confidence in one another's rather reticent company.

Then, I shifted my spying position and stepped several-hundred-feet over to a little knoll that gave me the advantage of a yard or more higher elevation, and when I frankly looked back for Johnson, presently, my former 'old geezer' companion was seen walking towards Maybury, still scratching his shriveled testicles.

The sunset faded to twilight before anything new and out of the ordinary happened. The Woking crowd to my far left seemed to be growing larger, and I heard a faint murmur of dialogue being generated from among the gathered gaggle. But to my right, the little knot of worried bystanders had dispersed in the direction and security of Chobham. However, during that brief interval, there was no observable activity or movement transpiring inside or around the accursed pit.

It was that lull, as much as anything else, that afforded the remaining spectators and myself new-found courage, and inspired our mutual intent and purpose; for together, we bravely approached the perilous hollow.

Then, being more relaxed and again feeling normally complacent, I noticed that a half-dozen accompanying cabmen had boldly paced-down into the sand-pit, and my ears soon heard the clatter of hoofs along with the grinding of wheels.

I noticed a lad casually trundling off the barrow of apples. And then, within thirty-yards of the dreaded, Martian-formed problematic pit, advancing from the direction of Horsell, I noted another bevy, actually a knot of idiotic pacifists, and the naïve marchers were foolishly pretending to be fair-minded local diplomats.

The foremost impostor foolishly led the phalanx forward towards the inhospitable alien cylinder, and the self-appointed ambassador was energetically waving a white canvas flag, symbolically representing either peace or surrender.

'What the fuck are those imbecilic knuckleheads doing?' I silently questioned. 'I'm certain that those nefarious Martians concealed inside that loathsome machine don't give two flying asteroids about our English customs, laws, ethics, values, LBGTQRSTUVW Community Weenie and Beef Roasts, religion, porno' mags, Magna Carta, S & M Sex and Tattoo Parlors, dildos, Parliament, Piccadilly Circus, Queen Victoria's Secrets, Westminster Abbey, London Body Mutilation & Torture Emporiums, Guy Fawkes Day, or even one scintilla about our sacred British Constitution!'

I later learned that at a combined emergency session of the Maybury Hill and Woking town councils, a hasty consultation had been organized, and since the Martians' crash had been officially verified, in spite of the aliens' repulsive forms, evidently, it was determined that the grey, amphibian-type alien fuckheads were intelligent creatures brandishing marvelous futuristic technology.

So, the cretin Maybury Hill and Woking politicians unanimously resolved to show the unfriendly spacemen, by using certain signals of peace and diplomacy, overtly demonstrate to the interplanetary encroachers that we citizens of Great Britain were also somewhat-intelligent and civil.

Flutter, flutter, went the improvised white Truce Flag, barely waving in the gentle wind, first to the right, then to the left. The peculiar event was too far away through the visible haze for me to recognize the blurred identities of any of the simpleton councilmen that had been dispatched from Maybury Hill and Woking, but afterwards, I had learned that Ogilvy, Stent, and Henderson were with several other quixotic dumb-shits who had been additional participants involved in that extremely precarious and ludicrous attempt at achieving communication.

Suddenly, there was a brilliant flash of light, and a quantity of luminous, green smoke wafted-out of the pit in three distinct puffs, which amazingly ascended like swirling miniature cyclones, one spiral after the other, straight into the still air.

The contaminating smoke (or flaming series of green illuminations) was so bright that the deep blue sky overhead, along with the hazy stretches of brown common stretching over towards Chertsey, seemed to darken abruptly as those odd puffs arose before eventually dispersing. At the same time, a faint, now-familiar hissing sound became audible, alluding that a wicked attack might soon be occurring, as is often the case with desert rattlesnake warnings here on Earth.

As the green 'tornado smoke' again billowed upward, as I recall, the peace party members' faces flashed-out pallid green reflections, and the jade color phenomenon gradually faded and then vanished.

Next, very slowly, the haunting hissing sound transformed into a low humming rumble, and finally, the tone evolved into a long, loud, droning noise. Slowly, and beyond belief, a humped shape rose out of the mystic hollow, and an intense beam of stimulated green light flickered-out from the strange mass's center.

Flashes of excessively hot flames, each thrusting-out a blinding bright glare, then strangely transformed into azure rays, leaping from one flare to another. Quite honestly, the alien activity scared the living shit out of me. Instantly, each quixotic councilman offering peace overtures was suddenly and momentarily turned into a mass of fire.

'These Martian octopuses are very dangerous, crazed maniacs!' I quickly surmised. 'Gay Attila the Hun and Genghis Khan of yesteryear were definitely more cordial and humanitarian! But now, Ogilvy, Henderson and Stent have all been evilly vaporized and fully disintegrated!'

I stood there motionless, staring, both shocked and mentally stunned, having great difficulty fathoming that the Martians' weaponry had so easily disposed of those three annoying assholes. And in a matter of seconds, the lethal 'humped cannon' whirled-around, and was soon directly targeting *my* ass, bent on also blowing me into unknown oblivion.

Feeling a dire need for survival, I leaped into a nearby trench and lay face-down with my open hands wrapped over my head. Several nearby coniferous trees instantly burst into flame, and every dry yew in the vicinity became ablaze. And far away towards the very popular unisex brothel over in Knaphill, my eyes witnessed the flashes of trees and hedges, along with the famous termite-infested, wood-framed unisex building suddenly set alight.

'Holy shit! Those luscious prostitute bushes over in Knaphill have met a similar fate to the scrawny yew bushes over here on the heath!' I regretted and concluded. 'Apparently, these totally fucked-up Martian invaders have some major grudge against local patrons paying for straight and gay sex! The satanic, extra-terrestrial monsters must be something akin to psycho, prudish Puritans!'

The amazing vengrance of the unbearable 'Heat-Ray' was now swiveling around and destroying anything and everything that existed within its extensive range. I sensed that the formidable 'death beam' was again pivoting toward me, as various shrubbery and deciduous trees in my proximity flashed and quickly burst into threatening flames.

My ears heard the close crackle of fire as screaming humans, sprinting like marathon runners from the distant sand-pit, turned green and ignited one by one, and my auditory perception heard the squealing of a plow-horse that was suddenly stilled by the all-too-powerful green Heat-Ray.

Then, as the humped cannon squeaked and rotated on its axle, my eyes confirmed that the immediate effect was as if an intense deadly gas had been egregiously demolishing every living thing in its path. Every plant, every tree, and every weed growing along the heath's curve-line smoked and crackled in a raging chorus of dissonant bursts. Several familiar buildings were horribly set on fire, and I recall my greatly-confused mind musing, 'I knew I should've worn my damned blazer!'

To my left, a distant flagpole toppled with a booming crash, approximately where the road from Woking Station opens-out onto the common. My abused ears soon recognized that the terrible hissing and humming had finally ceased, and the black, dome-like object sank slowly out of sight, being cunningly lowered into the foreboding hollow.

All of this fluid disaster had happened with such swiftness that finally, I weakly staggered to my feet, and my legs stood motionless inside the 'salvation ditch'. My thought processes had become dumbfounded and dazzled by the fantastic flashes of light that had viciously annihilated everything within its scourging influence.

Had that death beam swept through a full circle, it would have inevitably slain several dozen additional innocent bystanders. But the calamitous weapon had fortunately passed overhead and had luckily spared me from undeniable, vicious obliteration.

The smoke-veiled common then seemed spookily dark, except where its roadways lay grey and pale under the deep blue sky, with it being emblematic of early dusk. Overhead the stars and constellations were mustering, and in the west, the twilight sky was still a pale, bright, almost-azure blue. The tops of the pine trees and the roofs of Horsell then portrayed themselves as being sharp and black, being contrasted against the western afterglow.

The Martians and their catastrophic appliances had altogether disappeared into the pit, save for that thin mast upon which their restless mirror had wobbled, and the probing object, a sensor, evidently predicting the imminent utilization of the omnipotent 'Heat-Ray'. 'That raised tube must be some kind of periscope,' my racing mind theorized.

Patches of bush remnants, along with isolated scorched trees here and there, smoked and dimly glowed, and the distant houses near now-gloomy Woking Station were sending-up their normal chimney smoke into the evening air's eerie stillness, as if suggesting that everything was still quite normal.

To my mind's distorted interpretation, nothing in the way of regular life had changed in Woking, save for the terrible astonishment I felt in response to the cruel reality of what my disbelieving eyes had just witnessed.

'I'm lucky that my sinful ass had escaped being speedily sent into the afterlife!' I remember thinking. 'Just like the American Civil War General William Tecumseh Sherman's 'March through Georgia', those bellicose Martians must thoroughly enjoy practicing a ruthless, contemporary, British Scorched Earth Policy!'

It came to my feeble awareness that I had been hobbling about aimlessly upon the darkening public common, helpless, unprotected, and frightfully alone. Suddenly, a sense of fear and despair dominated and enslaved my confounded mind.

With a new effort, I turned my body and began clumsily stumbling through the somewhat-scorched heather, heading back toward my modest Maybury Hill dwelling. 'It's a good thing my shoes have thick soles,' I recall thinking.

The fear I felt was not rational, but instead, a powerful panic terror; yes, a sort of phobia. Not only was my brain imagining extreme apprehension regarding the dastardly Martians, but also, my damaged emotions were then enduring a new-found apprehension of the darkening sky, along with the inscrutable stillness that prevailed all around me.

I felt that every bit of testosterone had evacuated my throbbing testicles. 'My normally-high sperm count must now be quite depleted from narrowly escaping that recent misadventure!' my convoluted mind theorized. 'I strongly suspect that my precious epididymis must have suddenly atrophied!'

The sole favorable aspect of the entire deleterious ordeal was the essential fact that the hostile Martians had efficiently exterminated the toxic pestilence of Stent, Henderson and Ogilvy, whose grandson in later years had joined the Royal Air Force, and had informed me at a war memorial service that he had won first place in a national farting contest.

Without further hesitation or procrastination, I madly jogged toward Maybury Hill, weeping and shrieking as a spoiled child might do from his kitchen highchair. I had resolutely directed my aching legs to be bound for my much-desired residence, and I did not dare look back at the former chaotic scene.

I remember feeling an extraordinary emotional persuasion, a feeling that I had been played as a persecuted pawn by the utterly barbaric Martians. My brain was perplexed at considering the notion that the vile invaders had the capacity to afford me a mysterious death at their malicious pleasure, but the wanton fiends had elected not to do so. 'The wily bastards could've killed me!' I concluded. 'I do believe that they're scrupulously saving my execution for later!'

Chapter 6

"CHOBHAM ROAD"

It is still a matter of great wonder how the Martians were able to slay mortal men so swiftly and so silently. Indeed, there was nothing exquisite, dainty or delicate about either their rancid appearance or their sophisticated weaponry. Many London officials had thought that in some remote way, the aliens were proficient at generating an intense Heat-Ray mixed inside a high-tech chamber of absolute non-conductivity. That intense heat the invaders projected into a parallel beam against any object that the bastard ogres chose to incinerate, possibly by means of a polished parabolic mirror of unknown composition, much as the parabolic mirror of a regular coastal lighthouse projects a magnified beam of light.

And the scientific concept of Light Amplified through Stimulated Emissions of Radiation (LASER) is, in this industrial century, mere hypothetical science-fiction theory. But I must concede the stark reality that the vile reptilian Martians had, more-than-likely, skillfully mastered the sage esoteric implementation of LASER Heat-Ray technology.

But no scholar has absolutely proven these supposed, very complex, scientific details in definite terms. However, the Martians' secret method of disintegration had been horrendously accomplished and executed, and it was certain and agreed-upon that a beam of unknown particles represented the essence of the concentrated matter that had been remarkably converted into operative Heat-Ray energy.

Whatever combustible material that had been used and then flashed into flame at its precise target, and as a result, made lead molt and then run like water. The green beam softened iron; the white ray cracked and melted glass with impressive facility, and when either of the heat streaks focused upon water, the liquid compound instantaneously exploded into hot steam.

That terrible night on the heath, nearly forty people lay dead under the familiar zodiac formations, and scattered piles of ashes abounded about the very surreal pit. And a few charred skeletons had been cremated almost beyond recognition, and all night long, the common, from Horsell to Maybury Hill, had been deserted, and most every area was brightly ablaze.

The news of the horrific "pit massacre" probably reached Chobham, Woking, and Ottershaw at about the same hour. In Woking, the arcade shops had abruptly closed when the tragedy had been announced through word of mouth, and a number of people, attracted by the bizarre stories which they had heard, were walking over the Horsell Bridge, and then, also along the road between the hedges that ran-out in the direction of the common.

The obnoxious Woking teenagers had made the extraordinary Martian crash landing a cause for their curious investigation. The imaginative excuse that the insidious young thugs had perpetuated to their apathetic parents was that the group would be traveling on foot to the common, simply to engage in trivial flirtations and "making-out" at "the new passion pit".

"Well, Mollie. Let's have a terrific sex party over at the sand pit. We'll teach the Martians how we derive pleasure from our exciting voyage through puberty!" one juvenile piss-head suggested.

"Good idea, Angus," Mollie readily agreed. "If you pretend that you're an aroused bull in heat, I'll pretend I'm a receptive cow. There's a neat pasture over near the common where we can get laid!"

"Let's make it a threesome," Malcolm added to the dumb-ass conversation. "I think I'm ready to get my first erection!" the vernal idiot ejaculated. "I can't wait to get my noodle wet, even if it's lousy sloppy seconds! Let's get it on!"

As yet, of course, few people in Woking even knew that the sinister crashed cylinder had opened inside the pit, though poor deceased Henderson had smartly paid and sent a tri-sexual messenger, riding upon a brand-new bicycle to the town post office, with a special wire that had been addressed to his employer, an evening London tabloid.

As various Woking folks came-out by twos and threes upon the open area, the curious itinerants found little batches of countrymen talking excitedly and peering at the spinning mirror gyrating above the sand-pit, and the newcomers were, no doubt, soon infected by the general attraction of the occasion, while the more astute adults, suffering from erectile and clitoris dysfunction, gladly watched through binoculars the two-dozen juvenile couples getting laid in the cow pasture at the opposite side of the common.

By half past eight, there may have been a throng of three hundred rubbernecking voyeurs eagerly viewing a variety of teenage necking and orgasms, and that numerical adult count was besides those seven angry, pissed-off homosexuals, who despised witnessing heterosexual activity, and who had urgently left the road, cursing a litany of expletives after watching the teenagers strenuously humping and pumping.

There were three policemen on the scene, also; one of whom had been mounted upon a donkey, all three doing their best, under instructions from a lieutenant, to keep the public back, and deterring the gathered knuckleheads from ignorantly approaching the perilous cylinder. There was some booing and heckling being generated from those more-thoughtless souls from whom a crowd is always an occasion for producing irksome noises and moronic horse-play.

Stent and Ogilvy, before their unexpected demises, had telegraphed from Horsell to the local military barracks as soon as the Martians had emerged from their "meteorite machine". And the loyal royal soldiers were contacted and specifically instructed by the local bureaucrats, many of whom belonged to the ultra-liberal County Humane Society, advising the troops to protect those strange creatures trapped inside the cylinder from the pugnacious mob's escalating wrath.

After *those* dual fiascos had ensued, Stent and Ogilvy had stupidly returned to the infamous pit to lead that already-documented, ill-fated, dumb-shit White Flag advance. The description of their extraordinary deaths, as it later had been discerned by the current assembled crowd, tallied very closely with my own graphic impressions: in summary, the three puffs of green smoke; the deep humming dissonance, and the sensational flashes of orange flame all occurred in *that* three-phase *s*equential order.

But in the final analysis, that assembled, volatile crowd had a far narrower escape from disaster than I had previously experienced. Only the fact that a mound of heaped sand had intercepted the lower part of the Heat-Ray had saved their fat and skinny asses from immediate cremation. Had the elevation of the parabolic mirror been a few yards higher, none of the ignoramuses could have lived to ever re-tell the wild and crazy episode.

In the sudden thud, hiss, and glare of the igniting trees, the panic-stricken area imbeciles, all tightly held locked elbows for moral support. Their circular formation was fashioned around the pit, swaying back and forth at the very outset of impending tragedy.

Sparks and burning twigs began flagrantly falling onto Chobham Road, and even single leaves ignited like tiny fireworks' puffs. Hats, dresses, penises, assholes, and ladies' bushes all caught fire. Loud shrieks and shouts were futilely yelled, and suddenly, a mounted policeman came galloping upon a miniature pony through the chaotic confusion with his hands clasped over his head, screaming certain imperatives from his hoarse voice-box.

"They're coming!" a woman near me hollered. "Not in a sexual manner, mind you! They're fuckin' coming, with nasty vengeance to kill us all!"

Everyone in the throng was pushing and shoving at those individuals directly behind them, attempting to clear their way and escape back to the presumed safety of Woking. The majority of the throng bolted as if the nutcases were a flock of spooked sheep.

Where the Chobham Road became narrower between the high-sided banks, the incited, fleeing sprinters jammed and funneled through the diminishing width. And four persons, (two virgins, a pedophile rabbi, and a sex predator) perished after being crushed and trampled, and their injured anatomies were left to die upon the common, amid all the frenzied terror.

Chapter 7

"REACHING BACK HOME"

For my own part, I remember little of my evacuation flight except the stress of blundering against trees and stumbling through the thick heather. All about me was the intimidating, awesome Heat-Ray, zapping and flourishing overhead before the beam descended and vaporized my fellow citizens out of existence, as I came into the adjacent road between Woking and rural Horsell.

At length, I realized that I could go no further. I had become exhausted from contending with the external physical crowd violence, and from enduring my internal emotional struggle. I staggered, tripped and awkwardly fell by the wayside. My dreadful dilemma had occurred near the bridge that crosses the canal by the community gasworks. Being overcome with fatigue, I faltered upon the ground and lay still, where I must have remained prone for quite some time.

I suppose around fifteen minutes had elapsed, and I finally mustered sufficient strength to sit-up. For a moment, I could not clearly understand or remember exactly how I had arrived there. My previous anguish had fallen from my memory like a discarded garment. My fedora hat had gone, and my white collar had burst-away from its worn fastener.

A few minutes before my collapse, there had only been three real things my mind had clearly discerned: the immensity of the downed meteorite; my own feebleness and fright, and my fortuitous escape from death.

Now, it was as if my previous point of view about my important place in the vast Universe had been severely altered. There was no sensible transition from yesterday's passive state of mind to my present state of trauma. Just twenty-four hours earlier, I remembered being a decent, ordinary, happy British citizen. The silent common, the impulse of my flight, and the ascending flames, were as if those factors had been negatively experienced in a totally pathetic nightmare.

I soon pessimistically asked myself whether those recent precarious scenarios, pertaining to antagonistic space aliens, indeed had ever happened? In truth, my comprehension could not credibly synchronize the indecipherable connection between 'placid yesterday' and 'violent today'.

I gained my equilibrium and hobbled unsteadily up the steep incline leading to the sturdy stone bridge. All along the arduous trek, my mind had been saturated with blank wonder. My muscles, nerves, and kidneys seemed drained of their normal power, especially my kidneys, since I had inadvertently pissed-my pants three times out of sheer fright and flight.

A head rose over the bridge's crest, and the figure of a workman carrying a large woven basket appeared. Beside him ran a little boy, whom I assumed was the laborer's son. The two strangers passed me, wishing me "good night". I was minded to speak to the two courteous dipshits by saying: "What the hell's wrong with you boneheads? Are your brains inside your assholes?" Instead of answering their friendly greetings in sentence form, my lips produced a bland, meaningless mumble, and then thereafter, my aching feet conducted my hurting body over the bridge.

A multitude of pertinent interrogatives soon plagued my semi-consciousness. How could the Martians build a futuristic space vehicle, or become so scientifically erudite as to be capable of creating an obliterating Heat Ray? Quite obviously, the freakish species possessed no hands or flexible wrists to ever turn bolts and nuts with wrenches? 'Can the Martians screw without having nuts, or screw without wrenching their backs? Are the slimy killer vermin hermaphrodite lizards? Do the maniacal Martians know anything at all about either Hermes or Aphrodite in Greek Mythology? Do the invading fuckheads possess reproductive tits, pussies, balls and fadorkenbenders? Do the aliens indulge in reading juicy London porno' mags by means of advanced inter-planetary telecommunications?'

My pure concentration was rudely interrupted to my right when my attention had been directed to the Maybury train bridge's arch, where a speeding locomotive was then billowing a tumult of white fire-lit smoke, and my bloodshot eyes observed the long caterpillar of lighted windows passing southward with the all-to-familiar rail clatter. In the distance from the Woking Station, my auditory perception heard a loud group of irate citizens on the waiting platform, their throats vehemently screaming and cursing indiscernible histrionics.

Inside the locked gate to my left was a charming bungalow with exquisite gingerbread gables that just yesterday, had been an ideal abode in a quiet village called Oriental Terrace. My comprehension at that particular moment was rather calm, quite contrary to the abundant death and destruction left behind me at the pitiful pit! Everything in my mind seemed contradictory; either frantic or fantastic!

Perhaps I am a man of exceptional moods, and highly addicted to exaggerated sexual and eating appetites. I do not know how far my experience is, in any manner, common with the Martians' apparent lust for incessant, unwarranted killing. At times, my sensitivities suffered from the strangest feeling of detachment from myself, and also, isolated separation from the transformed, convoluted world around me.

My disbelieving eyes watched the ambivalent turmoil manipulating the overt actions and reactions of various people, all seemingly transpiring in a mass trance, and wildly milling around me. On that turbulent evening, the abnormal mental nemesis agitating my fearful mind was very strongly impacting upon my vacillating decision-making ability.

But the basic trouble was the blank unconcern, or general apathy, of many of the area residents, who persisted on pursuing their daily business without a worry or a care, possibly lacking thorough knowledge of the massive deaths occurring just a half-mile yonder. There was a noise of ordinary business from the gasworks, and the regular oil lamps were habitually lit in Woking. I paused and stopped to engage in serious conversation.

"What news from the common?" I asked two men and a woman standing idle outside the train station.

"Eh?" said one of the gentlemen, turning to answer my inquiry. "Are you daft, man? Have you been drinking Manhattans in London? Ha, ha, ha!"

"What news have you heard from the common?" I sternly asked the second male commoner.

"Ain't ya' just *been* over there? You came from that direction?" replied the bemused fellow. "Common sense ain't too common nowadays, that's what the hell I say!"

"People seem fairly silly about haunted night activities over in the common," answered and contributed the unperturbed woman. "What's the hubbub all about? Are you reading too many porno' magazines, or what?"

"Haven't you heard of the men from Mars?" I wanted to know. "The attacking creatures from Mars?"

"Quite enough," remarked the woman. "Thanks, but no thanks! Now, Stranger; I think you read both science fiction and porno' mags! Ha, ha, ha! Do you suffer from dementia? Ha, ha, ha!" And then, all three amused shitheads, ignoring the subject of Martians completely, indulgently laughed their conceited asses off.

I felt both foolish and angry after being so publicly mocked and ridiculed. I could not in good faith tell those three blockheads about the great human carnage and destruction I had seen. The idiots would have relentlessly laughed again and again at my broken oral sentences.

"You'll hear more yet about the invaders," I predicted. "And I'm not bullshitting about toy lizard-wizard dumbasses, either!" I reprimanded. And then I proceeded trudging in a melancholy mood toward the comfort of my mundane Maybury Hill home.

At my abrupt front door entrance, my wife was quite appalled seeing my haggard and unkempt appearance. I rapidly rushed into the dining room, sat-down, drank a quart of wine, and as soon as I could sufficiently collect my inebriated wits, I told Beatrice about the fucked-up events I had experienced.

"Let's have some decent sex!" my better half offered. "The gratification will make you feel better. I promise I'll make your non-fiction and porno' fantasies come true! On second thought, dear Husband, you're positively drunk, and I fear that your flaccid dick tonight will officially be known as Mr. Softy!"

The mutton dinner, which was a cold and tasteless one, had already been prepared and served upon the dining room table, and most of the meal remained neglected while I shared my crazy story, but soon, my bored and frustrated wife abandoned the room to go and privately read her own illustrated lesbian periodical in the parlor.

"There is one thing, Beatrice," I mentioned to her as she swiftly departed. "The Martians are the most sluggish things I've ever seen, including the slimy snakes crawling-about in stagnant swamps and local ponds. The huge slimy reptiles might keep the hollowed-out sandpit as an alien fort, and fanatically kill all curious people who come near their battlement!"

"Stop speaking your nonsensical drivel, my dear!" Beatrice replied and chastised. "I don't want to listen any more about the aliens' ugly features, or about their weirdo organisms and appendages! I'm more into vicariously enjoying reading lustful articles about intense, feminine self-induced climaxes right now."

"Poor Ogilvy!" I muttered to myself. "To think that he may be lying dead there, a mere heap of ashes; never again to ever fart, or stand erect, or work his erection!"

My wife did not find my Martian story credible. When I saw how deadly white her face was, I ceased lecturing abruptly, not aware at the moment that she had become completely exhausted from vigorously rubbing her engorged clit button, thus accounting for her very pallid facial complexion.

"They may come here," Beatrice replied again and again as she emphasized the word *come*." I've never had sex with an alien, and I don't plan on starting!" she insisted and declared.

I pressed for her to swallow-down a full glass of wine, and wanting to finger her bushy snatcheroo, I tried to allay my spouse's worry about being raped by Martians. "They can hardly move," I stated. "And I'll wager that the grey scum-wagons have no sizable dicks!"

I began to comfort my better-half by repeating all that Ogilvy had told me of the impossibility of the Martians successfully establishing their' presence in random Earth Colonies settled on all continents. In particular, I laid considerable stress upon the gravitational difficulty that the invaders would encounter. "On the surface of the Earth, the force of gravity is three times what it is on Mars," I explained, as I massaged her erect nipples. "A Martian, therefore, would weigh three times more than he or she would on Mars, albeit his or her muscular strength being affected. Don't you understand *that* basic principle?"

"What do you think the Martian women look like?" Beatrice seriously asked. "Worms or slugs?"

"I believe they'll look like writhing serpents and lizards, disguised as scurrilous reptiles," I answered. "The slimy freaks must reproduce by having sex in polluted swamps and stagnant bogs!"

Since Beatrice desired having no more intense orgasms involving me, I began considering some scientific conjecture. The atmosphere of the Earth, we now know, contains far more oxygen or far less argon (whichever way one likes to put it) than does the probable lighter air density on Mars. The invigorating influences of this world's excess of oxygen upon the Martians, indisputably, would do much to counterbalance the increased weight of their fucked-up bodies.

And, in the second place, I had erroneously overlooked the fact that such mechanical intelligence as the Martians shrewdly possessed was quite able to dispense with their using muscular exertion. The race seemed physically weak, relying heavily on bulky machines and advanced technology.

My reasoning at that moment was dead against the chances of the invaders ever succeeding at establishing a permanent colony outside the borders of Woking and Maybury Hill. With wine and food, and the satisfying confidence of my own living room, and also, the necessity of reassuring my sex-starved, nymphomaniac wife, I grew by degrees increasingly courageous and secure. Back in bed, I audaciously related to my cynical spouse my new analysis.

"They have done a foolish thing," I related to Beatrice, fingering my wine-glass and imagining that the object was her wet pussy being penetrated. "The Martians are dangerous because, no doubt, the insane lizards are mad with habitual killing and conquest. Perhaps the freaks expected to find no living things here in England; certainly, no intelligent living things that might resist their ambition to dominate and control our good Earth."

"Who gives a shit?" my wife challenged. "Have lousy sex with a slithering Martian reptile in your fuckin' sleep! That'll really give you erectile dysfunction for the rest of your life."

"I tell you, Beatrice. An army shell exploding inside the pit will kill them all," I maintained. "And it won't be a fuckin' peanut shell exploding, either!"

"You're so damned drunk that you won't be able to shoot any sperm juice out of your miniature cannon tonight," my wife rankled and chided. "Go the fuck to sleep and *dream* about having a damned white one! When you're inebriated like you are right now, confidentially, your tiny dick looks-like a deflated sausage!"

"Well then, Beatrice. How about just giving me a full body massage, minus my junk!"

Chapter 8

"FRIDAY NIGHT"

The most extraordinary development that had been perplexing my disarrayed mind, of all the strange tragedies that had transpired that Friday, was the dovetailing of our social order, meshing daily community activities simultaneously with the first series of helter-skelter events occurring on and near the common. The Martian interference into local British societal affairs was beginning to heinously shake and topple *this* aspect of England's social order.

If on Friday night a resident had taken a pair of compasses and drawn a circle having a radius of one-mile around the now-treacherous Woking sand-pits, I doubt if that person would have had one human being inside it, unless it were some greedy heir of deceased Ogilvy, Henderson, Stent, or a disconsolate relative of one of the three London-based workmen who had also been vilely incinerated upon the now-lethal common.

Many area citizens had heard about the destructive ray-beams produced by the sunken cylinder, and those people neurotically talked about the weapon's alleged potency in their leisure conversations, but it certainly did not extensively make sensational tabloid headlines that a war ultimatum issued by the Prime Minister to avaricious, warmongering Germany would have done.

In London that night, poor Henderson's telegram had described to the disinterested press the gradual unscrewing of the Ray-Gun capsule, which the editors prudently judged to be a blatant canard. And it was rumored that the haughty newspaper executives, after learning of their elite reporter's inexplicable demise, instructed the editorial staff *not* to print a special edition editorial depicting Henderson's instant cremation.

Even within the aforementioned one-mile imaginary circle, the great majority of the indigenous population was relatively inert and laconic about recent accounts of the "fantasy comic book Martian menace". All over the Woking red-light district, patrons, bisexuals, and even expensive ninety-year-old prostitutes were gaily dining and ostentatiously supping without much concern or worry that their fragile lives might be in jeopardy.

In Woking and its suburban outskirts, working men were returning home and performing gardening after the labors of the day, and their casual conduct obviously being in great denial of the incredible evils that were currently situated in the sandpit.

Whimpering children were being put to bed by carefree parents; young acne-faced assholes were wandering through the lanes and practicing love-making in backyard hammocks, and phlegmatic upper-school students were zealously reading enthralling porno' mags that were furtively concealed inside their open textbooks.

Maybe there was an occasional murmur in the beauty salons and in the barber shops about the Martian crash landing, with the scuttlebutt being communicated in the form of hearsay, also along the various village streets and in shady alleys. The almost-taboo "Martian subject" was indeed a novel topic in the often-visited brothels and nudist camps, and here and there, dashed several ambitious messengers, pretending to be Hermes or Mercury, acting as euphoric gazettes.

But for the most part, the daily routines of working, eating, drinking, sleeping, fornicating, and masturbating carried-on as standard exercises, which were treasured British traditions and loyally enacted at Woking, Horsell, Chobham and Maybury Hill, just as those habits had been traditionally honored for countless years, passed-on from generation-to-generation.

The public's "herd mentality" general deportment acted as though the planet Mars had no direct significance or relevance in the hedonistic residents' everyday lives, and the working-class folks believed that the tiny, red, celestial mass was merely a remote, academic encyclopedia matter that existed only in the night sky and in school science books.

In Woking Junction, until a rather late hour, trains were stopping and going on their routine nightly schedules; daily passengers were snorting opium; others were scratching their asses and impatiently waiting on the rickety wooden platform, and everything ordinarily regarded as being conventional and habitual was, just like clockwork, proceeding according to Hoyle in the most predictable way. The only reported irregularity was the daily London train line that leads to Leeds.

A freckle-faced newspaper hawker was peddling papers and cheap illicit drugs on the corner of Woking's main intersection. The ringing clatter of pushcart wheels, the sharp whistle of the engines from the bustling train junction, mingled with boisterous and exaggerated shouts of "Space Men from Mars!" caused much hilarity and amusement among passing pedestrians.

Eyewitness depictions of the devastating Heat-Ray massacre at the newly-formed sandpit the night before were scoffed-at and dismissed by skeptical and dubious listeners as being "silly travesty" expressed in the form of inane jabberwocky.

"I saw the blood-thirsty Martians' Death Ray kill at least seven people," one Woking observer reportedly attested. "It was both gruesome and macabre!"

"Are you an escaped mental patient?" a critical listener inquired. "I think you need to secure a bed in Bedlam!"

"And I also made a few killings yesterday, but they were in the stock exchange and not out on the common!" a snobbish businessman overhearing the Martian invasion description jested. "Naturally, my friend; the Martians out on the common are indeed blood-thirsty! The assholes are most-likely condemned and evicted vampires escaping from lenient prisons on the red planet! That theory I learned from some nineteen-year-old juvenile delinquent kindergarten kid! Ha, ha, ha!"

"But I swear I had witnessed the harrowing genocide at the sandpit over near the common with my own eyes!" the schizophrenic spectator loudly exclaimed.

"Your fuckin' eyes need to be examined by the county coroner!" the tall cynical financial investor retorted and laughed. "Oh well, Mr. Fiction! Here comes my delayed train to beautiful, metropolitan, slum-laden London!"

"Are you one of those bogus, starving science-fiction authors who my sex partner Gladys and I gossip about over at the Woking LBGTQRSTUVW clubhouse?" an obese five-hundred-pound hussy interrogated the worried Martian massacre eyewitness. "Are you a colleague of that fraudulent novelist H. G. Wells?"

Before getting beaten-up in a violent altercation, I gracefully turned-away from the escalating argument and stepped to a vacated section of the train station platform.

London-bound passengers peered and stared through the inside carriage windows, probably hoping to see the fat lesbian bimbo beat the shit and piss out of me; sit her obese ass on my face, and fart wicked tempest blasts of stench-laden intestinal gas up my vulnerable nostrils.

Looking to my right, towards the common, I noticed a certain flickering, and then several discernible sparks dancing-up from the direction of Horsell. An artificial red glow, along with a thin veil of dark smoke, had been drifting across the cloudless moonlit sky.

'Holy hurricanes!' I fearfully thought. 'The Martians are at it again, igniting heath fires; decimating cottages, and randomly slaughtering all British blokes and bitches within range of *their* horrid, rotating Heat-Ray. 'My eyes now see and understand that at least a half-dozen villas are burning like bonfires on *that* fringe of the Woking town border.'

There were lights aglow in all the houses on the common's right side of the three familiar villages, and the dismayed families living inside the independent households had kept their oil lamps lit all night long.

A curious crowd of worthless gossipers and panhandling mendicants lingered restlessly on both the Chobham and Horsell stone bridges. One or two of the more adventurous souls audaciously wandered-off and meandered-into the bleak darkness, and like braindead, doltish automatons, other dumb-shit idiots got on their knees and crawled near the Martian war machine, but unfortunately, their doomed asses never again returned from their extremely stupid enterprise.

Now and again, an azure-green projection, behaving similar to a warship's powerful searchlight, swept the expanse of the common, and my senses automatically anticipated that the detrimental Heat-Ray was ready to follow the Light-Beam's auspicious cue.

Save for such distant Martian illuminations, flickers, and flashes, most sections of the common were silent and desolate, and my astute mind adversely suspected that a new count of charred bodies and mounds of ashes would soon be strewn about under the apathetic stars.

The next morning, several constables, assigned to be on surveillance patrol, testified to the Woking Town Council that peculiar hammering noises had been lucidly heard originating from the awful Martian hollow.

So, that was the state of affairs as had been discussed Friday night by the Woking Council. However, in the center of the nefarious sandpit, the enemy cylinder rested, sticking into the skin of our precious Earth like a cannibal's poisoned dart. Around the Martian attack contraption was a lengthy patch of silent common, still smoldering in various places, and the enemy invaders, also inadvertently showing a few dim objects, possibly used for reconnaissance, and those unique and recent constructions had now been visibly erected, here and there, in a rather contorted triangular formation.

Beyond those fresh alien additions that had been introduced to the common by the stealthy, entrenched encroachers, lay the old, unsuspecting, British physical normality, along with the typical, unassuming country complacency.

The regular stream of daily life still innocently flowed as it had conducted itself for numerous decadent decades. The concept of the Martian Invasion was still understood by the skeptical area townspeople as being just a contemporary, asinine fairy tale.

The fever of war that would soon clog every Englishman's vein and artery; the truth that would convert every gullible idealist into a hardnosed realist, and the Martian challenge that would deaden nerves and make pacifists transform into callous volunteer soldiers, still had to evolve and develop.

All night long, the devious aliens were ambitiously hammering and busily stirring; being quite sleepless, determined, and indefatigable; and the horrible reptilians assiduously and obsessively performed their clandestine labor, building upon the machines which the relentless fiends had been making ready for conquest. And ever and again, foreboding puffs of greenish-white smoke whirled-up into the atmosphere to integrate into the starlit sky.

About midnight, a company of disciplined soldiers came through Horsell, and the troops deployed along the edge of the common, forming a military cordon. Later, a second company marched through Chobham to position on the north side of the partially alien-captured common.

Several officers from the Inkerman Barracks had been surveying the heath earlier in the day, and one, Major Eden, who had owned a splendid botanical garden near Croydon, was reported to be strangely missing. The ranking colonel of the regiment came to the Chobham Bridge and was busy questioning the crowd at midnight about certain sketchy details.

About eleven the next morning, the London tabloids finally acknowledged and gave credence to the "Martian Intrusion", thus indicating that fantastic science-fiction, had overnight, converted into genuine non-fiction.

A few seconds after midnight, the inquisitive Chertsey Road and Woking crowds observed a shooting star falling from the heavens, and then smashing into the adjacent northwest pine woods. The "comet" had reflected a greenish color, and had caused a silent glow, somewhat comparable to summer lightning. This anomalous meteorological event represented the stark appearance of the second Martian cylinder.

Chapter 9

"THE FIGHTING BEGINS"

Saturday that week is vividly etched in my memory as a day of enormous suspense. It was a day of lassitude too, hot and close, with, I had been reminded by Beatrice, a rapidly fluctuating barometer, suggesting the likely prospect of a much-needed rainstorm. I had slept little, though my wife had succeeded in annoyingly snoring and mumbling, and subconsciously, constantly moaning the names Archie, Sigmund and Ophelia. I rose from her oddball prattle and traipsed into my garden just before breakfast, and stood listening on my back patio facing towards the common. Little was audible except the stirring of a happy lark.

Archibald, the jovial milkman, promptly arrived as usual to deliver his dairy products. I heard the rattle of his dilapidated wagon, and I hustled to the side gate to ask the deliveryman the latest local news.

The reputed, twice jailed sex maniac related to me that during the night, the Martians had been surrounded by several hundred veteran troops, and that guns were expected to begin eradicating the villainous invaders that same evening. Then, my ears detected a rumble, which Archibald explained was an emergency express train transporting a regiment of military reinforcements to be later deployed at the destination sandpit.

"The Martians aren't to be killed," reported the milkman, "if that can possibly be avoided. The hospitals over in London want to examine the assholes to see if they actually do have assholes. Also," Archibald, continued, "the acclaimed doctors at the Dracula Institute over in bloody Liverpool desire to analyze the grey fucks' oddball protoplasm cells under microscopes, and if they're authentically green, further relevant research will be expertly conducted by St. Patrick's Leprechaun Hospital over in Dublin."

Later, I saw my facetious next-door neighbor, nicknamed Siggie, doing some early gardening, and I chatted with the semi-famous porn star/stage actor for a time, and then strolled inside my cottage to consume my regular cereal, tea and toast breakfast. Almost to my disappointment, it was a most unexceptional, dull and miserable morning. My snot-nosed neighbor was of the opinion that the troops would be able to either capture or destroy the weakling Martians sometime during the next twelve hours.

"It's a pity that the bloody aliens make themselves so unapproachable," Siggie rather vehemently declared. "Why can't the disgusting creeps be like that screw-happy whore over in Woking; Ophelia Honeywell, I believe, is her prestigious name! It would be interesting to know exactly how the Martians live, masturbate, and reproduce on their native planet; we might learn a thing or two about mastering some new sex positions."

Siggie came up to the fence and extended a handful of strawberries, for his garden fruit and vegetable sharing was as generous as was his known bordello "romper room" enthusiasm. Siggie, who often suffered from severe constipation, told me of the overnight burning of the dense pine woods near the Byfleet Golf Links, where the sex-addict used to become drunk and would occasionally get laid when uniformed girls from the religious Mary Magdalene Academy across the woods would also relish giving the hormone-driven bastard quality enemas.

"The blundering townspeople over in Woking insist," Siggie added, "that another one of those blazing meteors has fallen and rocketed into those nostalgic pines; yes, I believe number two."

"Number Two sounds awfully shitty to me," I remarked and chuckled. "Those spiteful piss-heads inside the metallic cylinder over in the sandpit have already done Number One!"

"But one's enough, surely," Siggie adamantly insisted, ignoring my cumbersome attempt at burlesque stage comedy. "I'll tell ya', Herbie. Those insane murders out on the common will cost the insurance people a pretty penny before everything's finally settled," the human sperm machine emphasized and then guffawed. "Will the killer Martians pay the final judicial decisions in *their* own legal tender? Do the grey fuckheads have any money system at all?"

The "fucking woods" were still burning, and Siggie pointed-out a haze of smoke billowing-up from where he used to pump the poop out of uniformed religious school sex kittens. "The Martians will be in hot pursuit of village people and macho men to torture and slay local citizens for days on end," Siggie stated in a saddened tone of voice. "And that dead as a crowbar Ogilvy still owes me fifty-five pounds of good money that the parsimonious fuck had borrowed to have delicious sixty-nine done with that vivacious bisexual whore, Samantha Goodhead, whose porn name is Ophelia Honeywell."

After breakfast, instead of busily working on my 'publish-or-perish' comprehensive university research paper on the subject of "Neanderthal Male and Female Homosexuality", I decided to amble-down towards the common to perform a bit of on-the-scene amateur detective investigation.

Under the railway bridge I discovered a group of imported soldiers, men wearing small round caps, while drinking early nightcaps. The chaps in the contingent were wearing dirty red jackets that were unbuttoned, and their garb was showing official-looking blue shirts, dark trousers, and black boots coming-up to the calves.

"Nobody except military personnel is allowed beyond this army checkpoint," the extremely-impulsive captain-in-command imperatively ordered to my face. "The sandpit over yonder is definitely off-limits to civilians like yourself."

"How are you going to defeat the invincible Martian Death-Ray?" I politely asked. "The disastrous beam will make you and your troops' disintegrated remains able to be distributed nationally in numerous churches around the kingdom next Ash Wednesday!"

"You're as funny as an asshole without an exit!" the insulted captain nastily scolded as the affronted officer reached for his razor-sharp sword. "Now get your ass the fuck out of here before I swiftly cut you a second anus!"

The martinet-like captain then nastily informed me that no one was allowed over the canal, and, looking along the road towards the bridge, I recognized that a sole army sergeant had been stationed there as a sentinel.

"I had seen the Martians inside the pit several nights ago," I articulated to the stern-looking sentry, who admitted that he once was a bear-hat Buckingham Palace guard for ten years.

"What the hell do the raunchy bastards look like?"

"A combination of lizard, reptile and slithering snake," I all-too-honestly answered.

"Sounds a little like my mother-in-law," the military policeman replied without exhibiting a smile or smirk. "We already have more-than-enough son-of-a-bitchin' swamp creatures infesting our polluted ponds, rivers, creeks, brooks and lakes!"

"How do you intend to fight them?" I wanted to know. "The shitheads kill all resistance upon first sight without any notice of an actual assault in progress. You'd better dig trenches and hide in the ditches because the baneful Heat-Ray only travels in straight lines, and cannot, to my knowledge, do a radical right angle turn downwards!"

"Thanks, for the essential information, pal," the austere sentinel replied. "I'll tell the Big Colonel in charge about your insightful advice. I've never been a rabbit or a hedgehog, but if I must dig a burrow in which to hide to save my pathetic life, then that's just what the fuck I'll do! I mean, who the hell knows what the next freakin' life might be like? Eternity might turn-out to be three times as bad as my present fruitless existence. Do the Martians have any necks, heads or faces?"

"The ones I saw squirm-around like psychotic octopuses," I sincerely related. "Just the sight of the gruesome freaks made me want to regurgitate my spleen and my duodenum. I've fuckin' had chronic diarrhea the last three days! But now, after I've nearly propelled my whole colon out of my asshole, I'm now friggin' constipated!"

"Sounds like your alimentary canal needs some elementary medical attention," the militant sergeant commented without ever cracking a grin. "Stop being a goddamned feckless civilian wimp.

You need to put on your big boy pants, eat more clams and oysters, and develop some intestinal fortitude!"

I left the austere sentinel's militant company and feeling quite despondent, I trudged back towards Maybury Hill, wondering if the demented Martians had bordellos and nudist camps on their red planet. 'Maybe their food supply was running out? Or perhaps radical changes in their atmosphere, or alternations in climate had necessitated their migration to Earth? Whatever the circumstances may be, if I ever have the opportunity, I want to savagely castrate the bastards and hang their balls above my mantel as well-deserved trophies. That is, if the fucked-up slimy reptilians have any damned testicles and penises to slice off!"

I was frustrated that I did not succeed in getting a decent glimpse of the common, for even the Horsell and Chobham church towers were in the hands of the London-based military authorities. The soldiers I had addressed didn't know any vital specifics about the Martians. I also found the people in the town were feeling quite smug and secure in the presence of the well-trained military, and I heard for the first time from Thomas Marshall, the raspy-throat tobacconist, that his impudent and disobedient son had been among the dead casualties incapacitated on the common. Martial Law had already been declared, and the enforcement soldiers had made the residents on the outskirts of Horsell lock-up and abandon their vulnerable houses.

I got back home to swallow-down lunch about two that afternoon, and my body was very tired, for the day had been extremely hot for that time of year, and in order to refresh myself, I took a cold shower, all the while imagining sharing a warm, soothing bubble-bath with sexy Samantha Goodhead, whom I only knew from explicit photographs published in one of my wife's cherished porno' magazines.

About half past four, I ventured-out to the railway station to purchase an evening paper from the young hawker, who mostly profited from being a cheap drug distributor. The morning editions had contained only inaccurate, nebulous descriptions of the killings of Stent, Henderson, Ogilvy, young Thomas Marshall, and the other Martian Heat-Ray victims.

Fresh attempts had been made to signal the enemies in the sandpit's cylinder, but the army could not communicate, with any degree of success, with the reptilian interplanetary visitors. That phony summary happened to be the same naïve stereotype that was being portrayed in the headlines of the dumb-shit London newspapers. Considering the fate of the bearers of the white peace overture flag, I then totally understood the gross incompetence that was starkly evident in modern-day journalism.

I must confess that the sight of all the imported heavy armament, along with the excess of strategic military preparation, greatly excited me. Contrary to my regular benign demeanor, my imagination soon became belligerent, and out of character. I conjectured defeating the sordid invaders in a dozen striking ways; something of my schoolboy dreams engendering strenuous battle clashes and gallant heroism from Ivanhoe, King Arthur, Robin Hood, William Tell, and Sir Lancelot in particular, soon came back into my mental faculties.

It hardly seemed a fair fight for our prepared troops to go up against and easily vanquish the doomed Martians, I wrongly conjectured. In my fraudulent thinking, the scummy grey vipers seemed very helpless, futilely plotting and trapped inside that confined, half-buried cylinder at the common.

About six o'clock in the afternoon, there began the thud of cannons occurring at measured intervals from Chertsey and Addlestone. I learned from bicycle couriers that the smoldering pine woods into which the second cylinder had fallen was being constantly shelled, in the hope of destroying that second object before it opened and spread more widespread havoc. It was only about six-thirty, however, that a field gun reached Chobham for use against the first Martian machine, which had crash-landed in the sandpit.

About seven in the evening, as I sat at tea with Beatrice, my wife and I were talking vigorously about the intense battle that had been advancing upon us. I heard a muffled detonation blasting from the common, and immediately thereafter, a ferocious gust of fire filled the distance.

Close upon the heels of that mortar bombardment came a violent rattling crash, quite near to our location, and that shockwave trembled the ground as if the Earth had been stuffed inside a gigantic, active salt shaker.

And starting-out upon the lawn, I saw the tops of the trees encircling the Mohammed Junior College campus burst into smoky red flame, and the steeple tower of the little Islamic Mosque slid-down into disintegrated ruin. The pinnacle of the landmark edifice had vanished in seconds, and the roof line of the nearby college dormitory looked as if a hundred-ton artillery gun had been blasting ample munitions upon it.

My home's chimney had cracked as if a direct shot had impacted it, and a hunk of red brick came flying in my direction, soon clattering-down upon the floor tiles, and the smash caused a heap of broken fragments to ricochet into the large flower pot situated by my study window.

Beatrice and I stood amazed, and together, gasped in speechless fright. Then, I realized that the crest of Maybury Hill where our home had been built must be within range of the Martians' destructive Heat-Ray, now that the Arab Junior College dormitory had been maliciously shelled.

I roughly gripped my wife's arm, and without speaking, ran her out onto the road. Next, I fetched-out my neighbor's domestic servant, instructing her that I would comfort the girl's heightened hysteria when matters would eventually calm down.

"We can't possibly stay here," I concluded and quietly communicated in an unnecessary whisper. "Our own inept soldiers are demolishing this very community."

And as I uttered those plausible words, the firing again reopened upon the common, making the aghast cleaning maid wildly bite my right wrist that had been wrapped around her shoulder, making the flesh bleed.

"But where are we to go?" Beatrice asked in terror. "We might actually be safer inside our house! I wish we had a friggin' bomb shelter built in the basement where the three of us could hide! Shit! We don't even have a cellar! If anything, I gotta' salvage my precious illustrated sex magazines in my private room!"

Reentering our cottage, I remembered my wife's wealthy cousins' place. The buffoons owned a lucrative soccer ball manufacturing company. "Leatherhead!" I shouted above the distant booming and blasting salvos. "We'll escape to Leatherhead!"

Beatrice looked away from me and directed her attention to the parlor window. Our astonished neighbors down the lane were seemingly shellshocked, and were scampering out of their houses, seeking more adequate shelter from the raining, misguided army shells.

"How are we going to get to Leatherhead?" my impetuous wife asked. "I don't want to make mediocre soccer balls if I ever live through this incompetent army artillery barrage!"

"Look, Beatrice. We'll dash the half-mile to the Spotted Dog Tavern," I directed. "I know the landlord, and the gent has several horses and dog carts which he leases as a side business for daily use. Jones will be unaware of the ensuing battle, and will gladly rent us a cart for the afternoon. I won't tell the dimwitted proprietor that we'll be heading to Leatherhead for refuge and actually staying there!"

A half-hour later, I approached the main counter at the dilapidated Spotted Dog Tavern. "I must have a pound," said Cedrick Jones, the burly landlord. "And I've no one available to drive the cart. Are you sure you aren't heading to the big soccer game tomorrow over in Leatherhead?" the dubious tavern owner suspiciously asked. "I've heard that it'll be quite a contest!"

"I'll give you two pounds," I offered and prevaricated. "I'm experienced at driving a dog cart. In fact, I was taught the useful skill by my uncle, Jack Union. I'll return the rental with full payment by midnight and promise that you'll be gaining a handsome profit," I predicted, with my left hand swearing upon a high stack of Korans, which Jones had recently obtained from the Mohammed Junior College!

"Lord!" hollered the volatile landlord over his dirty bar counter. "What's the fuckin' hurry? I'm selling my best bit of a newly-butchered pig. Only two pounds for the whole porker? What's your rush now?"

"Look, Jones. I'm quite thin at the moment because I lost a hundred pounds last week. I had some bad luck playing blackjack and poker inside a London casino!" I impulsively joked.

"Okay," Jones laughed. "That would make you a bad credit risk! Give me your two pounds! Then take the lousy dogcart and get the hell out of here before I change my suspicious mind."

I commandeered the rickety dogcart back to my home, loaded some valuables onto the rear bed with the help of Beatrice and the neighbor's gorgeous girl servant, and then I drove-off, seeing the newly ignited trees along the Oriental Village, all flourishing with tall orange-colored flames. Apparently, the implacable Martians had activated the deadly Heat-Ray to obliterate those parts of Maybury and vicinity. Looking back, the servant doll, who I would occasionally screw after we played "Doctor and Nurse", had been stranded behind.

"A thousand feet down the lane, an army soldier stopped my forward progress. "Cease and desist! You can't go further ahead. Instead, I recommend that you take the road northwest until you reach safety," the corporal suggested. "That deadly Heat-Ray is nothing like our best soldiers have ever seen or fought against! It fuckin' boggles the mind! It's really out of this world!"

The strict and serious fellow, whose scarlet red jacket was indicative that he had been a member of an elite army cavalier unit, abruptly turned, stared, and bawled something about "hideous octopus arms crawling-out from inside an oval casing that was shaped somewhat like a casserole dish cover".

And then, the spooked combat veteran began crying like a bratty toddler, and next, the highly-decorated war hero very energetically sprinted to a secluded valley lying beyond the crest of a nearby inflamed hill.

A sudden whirl of black smoke glided across the road had hidden the corporal's swift scamper for a moment. Confused, I turned around, and drove the dogcart back to Maybury Hill. And leaping from the driver's side and spraining my left ankle, I hurried across the lane to my neighbor's door and instinctively rapped to foolishly confirm what I already knew. From a note nailed on the front panel, I read that Mr. Fillmore and his kinky wife Elizabeth had fled to London for sanctuary.

I forgot about evacuating Fillmore and his horny wife, and hopped into the driver's seat that had been positioned next to Beatrice. In another moment, the two of us were clear of the irritating smoke and raucous shrieking, and our dogcart soon was heading down the opposite slope of Maybury Hill towards Old Woking.

In front of our approach was a quiet, sunny landscape; a rich farmer's wheat fields occupied both sides of the road, and the Maybury Inn, with its squeaky, swinging sign, was still unharmed. I noticed the town doctor in his cart speeding up ahead of me. At the bottom of the steep hill, I turned my head to once again gaze at the hillside I had been leaving.

Thick streamers of black smoke were shooting-up with threads of red fire, and the prodigious inferno was spiraling-up into the still air. The thick smoke already extended far away to the east and west. And the bumpy road had been dotted with screaming residents running like Olympic contestants towards Beatrice and me.

And very distinct, through the hot, quiet air, my trusty ears heard the whir of an army machine-gun, and an intermittent cracking of the latest model military rifles. Apparently, from random observations, the evil Martians were setting fire to everything within range of their indestructible Heat-Ray.

I am not an expert dogcart driver as I had fibbed to Mr. Jones, and I recall immediately turning my attention to the spooked cart horse. When I looked back again, the second hill had encountered black smoke and hot flames.

I slashed the distressed horse with the driver's whip, and gave the jittery animal a loose rein until our careening vehicle had escaped the surrounding turmoil. In my excited haste, my dogcart had overtaken and passed the more experienced local traveling doctor's standard mode of transportation.

"Where's Veronica?" I asked, referring to our neighbor's 'good-sex' servant.

"You again left her standing and crying back at Maybury Hill!" Beatrice replied.

Chapter 10

"IN THE STORM"

As the crow flies, Leatherhead is about twelve-miles due east from Maybury Hill. The scent of hay was in the air throughout the lush meadows beyond Pyrford, and the hedges on either side were sweet with multitudes of dog-roses. The heavy artillery firing that had broken-out while Beatrice and I were riding down Maybury Hill ceased as abruptly as it had begun, leaving the evening temporarily peaceful and tranquil.

We arrived at Leatherhead without further misadventure at about nine p.m., and the dogcart's horse enjoyed a full hour's rest while my wife and I ate a lousy pork chop supper with our two very argumentative cousins. So, preferring to face the lethal Martians than deal with our combative and insulting cousins, we rode the inferior dogcart back toward Maybury Hill to see if our cottage was still standing.

My spouse was curiously silent throughout the entire drive back toward Maybury, and seemed oppressed with apprehensive forebodings of lurking evil. I spoke to Beatrice reassuringly, pointing-out that the Martians were no doubt confined to the pit by sheer heaviness, and at the utmost, because of Earth's greater gravity, the dumb shits could not even be able to crawl-out of their mired-down entrapment.

But Beatrice, being wholly traumatized, answered only in irrational monosyllables. In the light of the moon, her face, I remember, was as white as a polar bear's fur.

For my own part, I had been feverishly excited all day. Something akin to the glorified, patriotic war fever that occasionally runs through a civilized society had penetrated into my blood, and in my heart, I was not so very sorry that I had to return to formerly placid Maybury that night.

I was quite hopeful that *that* last intense army mortar volley, which I had heard might have meant the welcomed extermination of the invaders from Mars. I can best express my state of mind by revealing that I truly wanted to be a grateful witness to *their* much-warranted defeat.

Our cynical soccer-addicted relatives had thought that our story of the Martians was an absolute canard, so the irritating brothers, 'Dubious Doug and Doubting Thomas', told us to get the hell out of Leatherhead and head back to Maybury to consult a psychiatrist, a young hawker drug dealer, and an avowed, experienced exorcist the following morning.

It was nearly eleven that night when I started *our* dogcart return home. My optimistic mind imagined that the Martian siege had dramatically ended. Overhead, the low clouds were moving fast past the moon, albeit not a breath stirred the lush wild foliage growing on both sides of the bumpy road.

Happily, I knew the Leatherhead main exit street intimately, and I recalled when growing-up, that my parents often referred to my thorough knowledge of regional lanes and maps as me being a "roads scholar".

"Do you think the Martians are now all permanently eliminated?" I asked my somewhat-shocked wife. "Do you think the attackers deserve to die without any negotiations or special justice trials?"

"I only know what I read in the porno' mags," Beatrice sobbed and uttered in her maudlin mental condition. "I only wonder how the disgusting species might reproduce with having all of those wriggling octopus-like arms. I mean, how could the species ever perform sixty-nine, let alone screw with numerous dangling tentacles?"

"You're right, dear woman," I concurred as I held tightly to the horse's reins. "For all we know, the males' dicks might be situated under their armpits, and the females' tits might be located inside their stinking assholes!"

I was a little depressed at first with the contagion of my wife's abundant fears, but very soon, my thoughts reverted to the Martians' fate inside the hollow; and also, I considered *their* presence in the forest where Siggie had enjoyed gratifying sex with the voluptuous religious school babes.

At that inordinate time, I had been completely in the dark as to the outcome of the evening's interplanetary fighting, and I was not even slightly cognizant of the vague and nebulous circumstances that had precipitated the monumental conflict.

As I came through Ockham (for that was the way I had returned, and not through Send and Old Woking), I became aware of, along the western horizon, a blood-red glow, which as I drew nearer, crept slowly up the sky. The drifting clouds of the gathering thunderstorm had been stunningly mingling with masses of black and red smoke originating from distant fires.

Ripley Street, believe it or not, was deserted, and except for a lighted window or so, the village showed no signs of pedestrian street life, whatsoever. Losing my normal concentration, I narrowly escaped an accident at the corner of the road to Pyrford, where a knot of jabbering blokes stood in the dark with their backs to the dogcart. The arguing residents communicated nothing to me as I passed, but Beatrice, who had partially regained her wits, was happy that we weren't mugged and robbed by "roguish vampires and night stalkers who were holding a demonic midnight vigil."

From Ripley Street, until I drove through Pyrford, I was in the valley of the Wey, and I feared that there might be 'no way out'. As the dogcart ascended the little hill beyond Pyrford Church, a distant glare came into view, and the trees about me shivered with the first intimation of the predicted storm that was approaching. Then, I heard the midnight church bells pealing-out their melodic tones from Pyrford, and next came the much-anticipated silhouette of Maybury Hill, with its tree-tops and roofs black and sharp against the eerie red background.

Even as I beheld that desirable image of my home village, a lurid green glare lit the road and brightly illuminated the distant woods towards Addlestone.

"Look over there!" Beatrice directed my attention to the right, distracting me from my helmsman duty. "It's the third meteor about to smash into the woods!"

"The Martians are sending reinforcements, and possibly additional supplies," I replied. "The planet wars are not over yet, by no means! I'll bet my meager life savings that the new alien ship is *not* delivering stoves, sinks, fish and chips, clothes, and welfare meals!"

Observing the third meteor's descent, its hue was blindingly violet, contrasted to the orange streaks of the thundering storm above. The first lightning flashes danced-out in an array of wild patterns, and the overhead thunder burst echoed like resounding rocket blasts. The formerly obedient horse became spooked; its aged teeth crunched-down upon the bit, and incredibly, the affected animal cooperatively bolted ahead.

A moderate incline runs towards the foot of Maybury Hill, and down the opposite slope, our ancient dogcart clattered and rumbled upon the familiar cobblestones. The thunderclaps, each seismic boom treading on the heels of another, sounded more like the working of a gigantic electric engine than the usual detonating reverberations that human ears would ordinarily perceive. The flickering celestial lightning was both blinding and confusing, and a thin hail gustily careened off our defenseless faces, as I strenuously piloted the cart down the hill.

At first, I regarded little of the external turbulence and focused my primary concern on the road before me. Disregarding the pelting hail, along with Beatrice screaming louder than when she would be having her finest orgasm, my attention was soon arrested by something mysterious that had been rapidly moving down the opposite side of Maybury Hill.

Upon initial impression, I theorized that 'the elusive mirage' had been a reflection of a house's wet roof, but one flash followed another, showing the apparition to be in swift, bewildering, rolling movement.

And this 'gargantuan Thing' is what I amazingly saw! How can I describe it? An intimidating monstrous tripod, higher than many London edifices, striding in a marked cadence over and through the young pine trees, and smashing the oaks and elms alike aside as if that loud destruction was its programmed purpose. The horribly stupendous contraption was some sort of walking robot, fabricated of glittering metal, and striding with total precision across the dense forest environment.

Articulated steel-like ropes were dangling from its center, and the rhythmic clattering of its passage frightfully mingled with the overhead violent thunder. A fierce flash came-out of a side portal rather vividly, heeling over the eastern horizon, only to vanish and reappear almost instantly, as it seemed, with the next awesome discharge, landing a hundred-yards away, and positively destroying a grain storage warehouse.

Can you imagine a milking stool tilted and then indiscriminately and violently bowled along the ground? That was the general impression that those instant catastrophic machine flashes gave me. But instead of a milking stool, imagine the juggernaut being a massive bodied war machinery, perhaps an aerial tank, resting upon a tripod stand, and shooting a barrage of electric mortars and green Heat-Ray beams all over creation.

"What the hell is that monstrosity?" Beatrice screamed like a mental patient strapped inside a straightjacket. "I've never seen anything so goddamned hideous!"

"It's some sort of Martian elevated, mobile fort," I surmised and rhetorically explained. "Whatever it is, it's far worse than getting bombed at Mr. Cedrick Jones's pathetically grimy Spotted Dog Tavern, that's for damned sure! Honestly, Beatrice. There're other more civilized ways that I'd like to have a blast!"

"The Martian invasion is no longer a reckless conspiracy theory circulating around Maybury," my wife verified as she finally and almost-magically harnessed her good senses. "These alien lizards, or vampires, or zombies, or whatever the heck the moral-less fucks may be, are out to erase us right off the face of the Earth. My intuition tells me that we should duck-down until we reach our humble home; that is, dear Herbert, if our lovely cottage hasn't already been callously shattered into cinders!"

Then suddenly, the trees in the pine wood ahead were parted by the awesome green Heat-Ray, as brittle reeds were also inexplicitly parted, and the various coniferous limbs and branches were snapped-off and driven headlong. And much to our accelerated horror, a second huge tripod appeared, rushing it seemed, at full throttle towards us.

At the sight of the new colossal mechanism, my nerves became even more twisted and jangled. Not stopping to look again, utilizing the black leather reins, I wrenched the exhausted horse's head hard around to the right, and in another moment, the dogcart had heeled-over, landing full-weight upon the fatigued equine; the riding wagon's shafts smashed noisily onto the road, and my wife and I were mercilessly flung sideways, our bodies being heavily deposited into a shallow pool of stagnant water.

Garnering my wits after re-gaining consciousness, I crawled-around inside the muddy ditch almost immediately, and then, standing in the mucky water, I crouched my feet, frightfully hiding my ass under a clump of thorny furze bushes.

The horse lay motionless (its neck had been broken, poor brute!), and by bursts of light created from the consecutive lightning flashes, my eyes eventually viewed the black bulk of the overturned dogcart, along with the silhouette of a detached overturned wheel, still slowly spinning. In another moment, the terrorizing Martian destructive mechanism went striding by me, and the incredible apparatus methodically passed uphill, going towards Pyrford.

'My goodness!' I conjectured. 'Even the irreverent-but-revered Woking Gay and Lesbian Sex Exchange is in imminent jeopardy of being incinerated in a widespread downtown conflagration!'

Seeing the immense device maneuvering ahead rather clearer, the object most certainly was an incredible war machine, steadily moving with a ringing metallic pace, and featuring long, flexible, glittering tentacles (one of which had gripped a young pine tree), swinging and rattling the selected timber as if exhibiting unbridled animosity.

The mobile fortress picked its path as it was mechanically striding along, and the brazen hood that surmounted its crown moved to-and-fro with the inevitable suggestion of an intelligent alien head, making clever and incisive decisions.

Behind the hulk's main body was a huge mass of white metal reminiscent of a gigantic fisherman's basket, and oddball puffs of green smoke squirted-out from the 'knee and elbow joints' of the massive instrument's substitute arm and leg appendages, and as the doomsday invention swept by, it was undoubtedly searching for convenient humans or houses to cruelly eviscerate.

When the moving fort passed my crouched position, it released an exultant deafening howl of "Atoo! Atoo! Atoo!" that essentially drowned-out the loud natural thunder and heavy rain of the raging storm.

And much to my alarm, in another minute, around half a mile away, the intimidating metallic contrivance had rendezvoused and joined its duplicate companion, each then stooping-over some unidentified item lying in the empty field. I have no doubt that this anonymous Thing embedded in the previously vacant ground had been the third elongated cylinder which the fiendish alien reptiles had deliberately fired at Earth from Mars.

I desperately searched the surrounding area for my beloved Beatrice, but my distraught mind guessed that my wife had probably wandered-off, and being in debilitating shock, was more-than-likely frightfully staggering in an unknown direction, in all likelihood to discover a satisfactory place of momentary refuge.

For some minutes, I knelt there in the trench, quite still, and needless to report, soaking wet in the rain, shivering in the nocturnal darkness. I was seriously watching, by the intermittent moonlight, those insensitive and brutal metallic beasts moving about in the distance, over and beyond the shadowy hedge tops.

My emotions anguished at the thought that Beatrice had possibly been slain or captured by the brutish reptilians. 'Who the hell knows what a Martian rape of a British woman would be like?' I imagined and cringed.

It was some time before my blank astonishment would permit my convoluted brain to think properly. Several critical minutes had elapsed, and I decided to struggle up the muddy swamp bank onto a drier position, where I could better contemplate my imminent peril.

Not far from me was a little one-room squatter's hut, rudely constructed of wood, and the isolated shack being surrounded by a weed-infested potato garden. I lifted my filthy frame from the mudbank, and then crouching and walking like a wounded duck, I courageously raised my head and made a mad dash toward the ramshackle shanty. My bleeding fists hammered at the door, but I could not make the presumed occupant inside respond to my futile beckoning.

Being exceptionally confused and under duress, pretending to be a turtle, I slowly crawled my way back to the familiar ditch, realizing that the deep trench meandered left and right, most of the way to Maybury.

I pushed ahead on my knees, while experiencing excruciating pain in my fists and aching shoulders. And being drenched, and in a disheveled state of mind, I advanced for several hours back towards my own house. Being tired, and with major agony throbbing all over my hurting body, I bitterly fell, rose to my feet, and then stubbornly stumbled and hobbled along a foliage-laden trail that ran parallel to 'Siggie's exotic and erotic sex woods'.

'Poor Beatrice,' I lamented. 'I already miss her dearly, despite her adverse addiction to reading those fucked-up, graphic porno' mags!'

Being quite unkempt and disoriented, I realized that I should have immediately wended my irregular way through Byfleet to Street Cobham, and so gone back to possibly rejoin my delirious wife, who was probably in a daze, more-than-likely heading back in the direction toward our fickle and temperamental 'soccer cousins' over in Leatherhead.

I had a strong desire of going onward to seek safety in my own house, and despite my abundant pain and suffering, I had been very curious to learn if the cozy domicile was actually still habitable. I staggered through the tall, charred trees, slipped again, bruising my knees against a downed spiked plank, and my weary legs finally managed to splash-out into the familiar lane that ran down from the College Arms.

I had mentioned the nomenclature 'splashed', for the torrential storm water had been sweeping the sand down the hill, with the erosion causing a muddy muck. There, in the ominous darkness, a man blundered into me, and the force of his collision sent me reeling back against a juniper bush.

The distressed fellow gave-out a pitiful cry of terror, sprang sideways like a scared jackrabbit, and rushed forward as in the manner of an incensed bull, even before I could sufficiently gather my wits to speak with him. So heavy was the stress of the relentless storm that I had the hardest task to resume my arduous trek up the hill.

Near the top of a familiar knoll, I blundered upon something soft, and, by a coincidental flash of lightning, my pupils noticed between my feet a heap of black broadcloth, along with a pair of leather boots. Before I could distinguish clearly how the prone fellow's bloody head and feet were aligned, the flicker of electric light had passed *our* position.

I stood over the man's limp form, anxiously waiting for the next lightning flash to illuminate the area. When it came, I recognized that the victim was a sturdy man, cheaply, but not shabbily dressed; his blood-stained head was bent under his dead body, and his corpse was lying crumpled-up, close to the nearby fence, as though the unfortunate bloke had been violently flung against it.

Overcoming the repugnance that is natural to one who had never before touched a cold, dead body, in hope, I stooped and turned the gent over to feel for a heartbeat. The coldness of his hand immediately communicated that the inanimate fellow was indeed quite deceased. Apparently, the victim's neck had been broken, and his cranium cracked, both probably being received from a huge falling tree limb.

Soon, the lightning flashed again, and the man's bearded face seemingly leaped-out upon me. I sprang to my feet in great dread. The visage that my eyes perceived belonged to Mr. Cedrick Jones, the obese landlord of the Spotted Dog Tavern, whose dogcart conveyance I had recently rented.

I gingerly stepped over his morbid corpse and determined that I should doggedly push-on up the hill. I made my way by the police station and next, by the College Arms, gradually ambling my way towards my once-happy dwelling. Nothing was burning on the hillside, though from the distant commons, there still came a red glare, and a rolling tumult of ruddy smoke, graphically clashing against the pelting hail.

As far as I could distinguish by the latest sequence of storm flashes, the houses about me were mostly intact and undamaged. However, by the local College Arms, a dark heap lay in the road, which I assumed represented the remnants of an overturned passenger carriage.

Down the road towards Maybury Bridge, there were voices yelling, but I lacked the wherewithal and strength to shout back, or even go interview the screamers. I let myself inside the cottage with my latchkey; closed, locked, and bolted the wooden door; awkwardly staggered to the foot of the staircase leading to the loft, and sat-down to rest my weary bones.

My imagination neurotically commenced reviewing those indomitable, striding, metallic monsters, and also, the dead body of Cedrick Jones that had been violently smashed against the warped fence. Realizing the scope of my escalating dilemma, and my mind, being a total mental wreck, my consciousness succumbed, and my spirit surrendered to fatigue. I soon fell to the floor, and my faltering awareness entered into a deep slumber.

Chapter 11

"AT THE WINDOW"

I have already explicitly stated how my mercurial tempests of ascending and descending emotions had developed an elusive trick of oddly exhausting themselves. After a short interval of mental numbness, I soon discovered that I was cold, wet, and depleted. And after awakening from my brief siesta, while holding the stairs banister, I managed to stand erect, with a little pool of water visible upon the parlor's red and black carpet. Then, subconsciously imitating the Martian machines, I mechanically staggered into the dining room and drank some potent rye whiskey, and next, my oscillating finite brain instructed me to the downstairs master bedroom to change my dirty clothes.

'This Martian besiegement is far worse than the scourges of cancer, diabetes, heart disease, paralysis, and all of the most detrimental earthly diseases combined,' I sadly assessed. 'And the worst is yet to come with the rule of public law and order soon converting into mass anarchy, and if there is a multitude of these satanic machines landing and creating disorganization and chaos all over the world, then the human race will quickly be reduced to savagery and cannibalism. And mortal beings will inevitably transform into our own evil enemies. In a matter of weeks, we'll all be reduced into contentious clans of primitive Neanderthals, or at best, Cro-Magnons, seeking group survival and security in available caves!'

After changing clothes and contemplating those grotesque scenarios, I stepped into my study, but why I did so, my faulty reasoning still cannot fully explain or reckon. My office's window looks-out over the distant trees and toward the railway line leading past Horsell Common. In the hurry of *our* hasty departure to Leatherhead, this particular window had been left open. Peering outside, I realized that the wild storm had passed, and I falsely hoped that the Martian invasion had been a cruel nightmare. My disbelieving eyes instinctively glanced at my lacerated fists and instantly comprehended that the alien aggression was indeed *not* a blatant hoax.

The towers of the local Mohammed Junior College and the pine trees about it had vanished into history, and very far away, lit by a vivid red glare, the once lazy common encircling the sand-pits was barely visible. Across the formerly-pristine scene, huge black shapes, grotesque and ominous, moved busily hither and thither like coordinated ants, dutifully servicing the needs of their colony.

'This alien shit that's going on out there is absolutely nauseating,' I evaluated. 'I dare not eat breakfast, fearing that I'll vomit my fuckin' guts onto the floor. I feel like stepping outside and poisoning the back-yard well, but I don't have any arsenic or hemlock stored on the premises,' my weakened brain whimsically considered as I weighed the notion of committing suicide and possibly winding-up in Anglican Hell as a substitute for the living hell that the heinous Martians were establishing.

It seemed indeed as if the whole countryside in *that* direction of accursed Horsell Commons had been maliciously set on fire, but I realized that the fucked-up Martians were much superior in creating mass devastation than ordinary British pyromaniacs or regular London arsonists could ever be.

A broad hillside, aglow with minute tongues of sparkling flames, which were swaying and writhing with the moderate wind gusts, was throwing a red reflection against the slowly-gliding clouds. Every now and then, a haze of pungent-smelling, gritty smoke drove across the open windowpane, and occasionally hid the partially-obscure Martian shapes.

I could not see and interpret exactly what the sinister invaders were doing while utilizing their futuristic equipment, nor could I distinguish and recognize the tall, black, in-motion objects that I presumed were alien derricks, or perhaps functioning cranes.

Nevertheless, a sharp, malignant, distasteful odor, similar to that of an ongoing widespread forest fire, was prevalent in the air.

I soon directed my visual attention to the opposite direction. My view reached to the houses in the vicinity of Woking Station, and on the other side of that angle, the site changed to the charred and blackened pine woods of Byfleet. There was a light shining down below the hill, on the railway, illuminating near the landmark arch, and several of the abodes along Maybury Road were now dots of glowing ruins.

The light upon the railway puzzled me at first; it was beaming from a black mound accompanied by a vivid background glare, and to the right of that spectacle, a row of yellow oblongs, which I also failed to identify. Then, my alert pupils recognized that the black object was a totally-wrecked passenger train, with the locomotive smashed and ablaze, and the tilted carriages apparently still canted upon seemingly warped rails.

'This bullshit carnage has got to stop,' I tensely concluded. 'Our most-modern cannons and other weapons are like kindergarten toys compared to the existence of fantastic Martian science and technology. I would attempt castrating the fucked-up bastards if I only knew what the hell I should be castrating!'

Between those three main centers of light exposing the burnt houses, the disabled train, and the blazing county buildings towards Chobham, irregular patches of dark country spaces were visible, broken here and there by intervals of dimly-glowing and smoking pastures.

It was the strangest spectacle imaginable. At first, I could distinguish no men or women milling-around, or hastily scampering anywhere. But later, I witnessed near the dull light of Woking Station a number of black figures, presumable brave repairmen, hurrying one after the other across the recently warped railroad tracks.

'And this was the wonderful little world in which I had been living securely for many years!' I recollected. 'But now, it's a gruesome, fucked-up, fiery, chaotic debacle! What other specific tragedies had happened in the last seven hours I still do not fully know; nor do I precisely desire wanting to know.'

My convoluted mind was stubbornly set to putting the puzzle pieces together as my educated, academic brain was beginning to connect the relationship between those mobile 'Martian killing-machines' and the sluggish lumps I had seen disgorged and quickly assembled from inside the original downed cylinder.

With a queer feeling of impersonal interest, I turned my desk chair to the side window, carefully sat-down, and pensively stared at the blackened country, gazing particularly at the three gigantic black 'things' that were operating in perfect tandem in the gloomy glare, seemingly hovering above the sand-pit.

The shithead aliens seemed amazingly busy conducting their secret activities. I began asking myself what the dangerous bastards could be satanically scheming and ruthlessly executing. Were the mechanisms intelligent on their own, or were the uncanny devices merely sophisticated, programmed robots? Or did an unscrupulous, immoral Martian sit within each contraption, ruling, directing, and using arcane technology, much as a man's brain sits and rules the myriad activities occurring both inside and throughout his mortal body?

I began comparing the abominable 'things' to rudimentary human-devised inventions, and I asked myself how an ironclad battleship, or a steam engine, would seem to a lower animal like a baboon, gorilla, or chimpanzee, or to any other separate branch of the Simian species.

The storm had fully departed from the early dawn sky, and over the smoke of the still-burning hinterland, the little fading pinpoint of planet Mars was predictably dropping into the western horizon, when all of a sudden, I viewed an alarmed soldier of the army division enter my garden. I heard a slight scraping at the fence, and rousing myself from my listless lethargy, I studied the uniformed man, dimly clambering over the palings.

At the sight of another viable human being, my former apprehension passed, and I leaned-out of the nearby window and eagerly addressed the mortal trespasser.

"Hey there!" I exclaimed. "What the fuck's going on out there on the common, and also in Woking? It appears that the pugnacious Martians are easily kicking the military's puny asses!"

The soldier ceased striding and halted his parallel path along the fence, and ceased carefully rummaging along the property. Then, coming over and across the lawn to the corner of the house, the possible deserter bent-down and spoke softly.

"Who's there?" the private whispered, standing under the window and seemingly peering-up at a ghost, namely me, Herbert George Wells.

"Where the hell are you going?" I curtly asked. "Are you seeking sanctuary and shelter? Are you a scumbag coward? If so, I don't really give a shit! I need the company of someone of my own British race!"

"Yes, on all counts!" the shellshocked AWOL soldier bluntly admitted. "I don't want to harm or kill you! I'm a loyal British enlisted man who has lost his way after my company had been scathingly excoriated by the atrocious aliens. Can you provide me a decent meal?"

I rushed to the front door, unfastened the lock, let the soldier inside, and quickly turned the key to the right. I could not see his full face, but noticed that the army private was hatless, and that his jacket was unbuttoned.

"My God!" the young gent exclaimed, after I allowed him inside. "Where in God's name am I?"

"What the hell has happened out there?" I sternly asked. "To tell the truth, you look pallid, like you've been circumcised at least five times!"

"What hasn't happened?" the army greenhorn replied. "Everything imaginable has gone awry! We don't stand a snowball's chance in Hades to defeat those demonic barbarians! If you have any hemlock or arsenic stashed-away in this house, I'll eagerly swallow-down a gallon of the toxic liquid!"

"Don't be absurd!" I orally countered. "Life is worth living, even though right now it might seem that such an attitude is erroneous! Tell me your battle story, and I'll determine if it is meritorious, or if it's deserving of a military court martial."

In the dull obscurity of the foyer, I still could interpret his gestures, all indicating grief and despair. "They wiped us out; simply wiped us out," my shivering guest repeated again and again. "Our finest and newest cannons are like a child's gadgets to them! It's like a toddler's cap guns going-up against their adult dynamite sticks!"

I soon learned that my new friend was quite intelligent and had been planning to enroll into Cambridge University for the fall semester, but needed to apply for an academic scholarship, and consequently, had voluntarily joined the army to earn tuition money.

"I looked on the brighter side of the matter because then I could save a few pounds to pay towards my college education," the young private intimated.

The beleaguered military rookie cautiously followed me into the messy dining room. His pale face was still ashen and smeared with battlefield grime.

"Drink some delectable whiskey," I offered, pouring-out a double dose. "This amazing shit will cure any fellow's erectile dysfunction, that is, if the powerful crap doesn't first kill-off all of your ornery sperm cells!"

The novice soldier quaffed-down the flavorful liquor in three gulps. Then abruptly, my passive visitor sat-down before the cluttered table, put his head on his arms, and began to sob like a spoiled little boy, while I, with a curious forgetfulness of my own recent melancholy, supportively stood beside his chair, wondering what revelations the distressed young man was about to confidentially divulge.

It was a long time before the army private could steady his nerves and answer my poignant questions, and then in a jittery fashion, address and satisfy my litany of inquiries. I learned that the private had been a troop transport wagon driver in the artillery battalion, and had only been introduced into action upon the common only one day before.

At that time, constant cannon firing was going on across the grassy landscape, and it was reported that the initial contingent of Martians had been meticulously and slowly moving-around in enviable motorized land vehicles, with the adamant shits scrupulously advancing towards their second crashed cylinder, under cover of a colossal, mortar-proof, metallic protective shield.

Later, I gleaned from the soldier's remarks, an exasperating shield had staggered-up like a child's musical jack-in-the-box, rising from sturdy tripod legs, and the contrivance became the first or second of the fighting-machines I had learned about, operating outside the sandpit.

"The gun which I was then assigned to deliver, had been unlimbered near Horsell, in order to take command of the sand-pit cylinder, and its arrival upon the common is what, I believe, actually precipitated the frenetic Martian reaction," the depressed soldier verbally reviewed and then paused.

"Tell me more," I honestly demanded. "Kindly describe your dipshit participation in the losing battle."

"As the limber gunners went on command to the rear, my wagon-horse trod into a large rabbit hole and faltered, swiftly throwing me into a narrow gully. At the same moment, the fuckin' harnessed gun exploded behind me, and the ammunition cargo blew-up the wagon. There was fire and plenty of chaos all around, and I found myself lying under several charred corpses, and also underneath the dead horse, since I had been quickly propelled off the transport wagon by the tremendous blast."

"Well, what happened next?" I insisted on knowing. "This perilous invasion is far from being a preposterous clown-show, you know! Tell me, Sir. Did you crap and piss your pants? Did you see the Martians up close? Were there any noticeable female aliens romping around on the battlefield?"

"I lay perfectly still, worrying that my pecker and testicles had been excised-off my torso. Scared out of my wits, with the gross weight of the wagon horse laying atop me, I fathomed right-off that a large segment of my company had been horribly extinguished by a self-inflicted tragedy. And the harsh smell of smoldering bodies, good God!" recently introduced Private Henry Morgan exclaimed. "The odor stunk like burnt barbecue meat roasting on a hot fire-grate!" the jinxed deserter disclosed. "I was hurt and lacerated all across my back by the fall of the weighty horse, and there I had to lie until I mustered sufficient stamina to wriggle-out of the pile, and to rise and seek adequate safety."

"You say you were wiped-out?" I asked.

"Wiped out!" Private Morgan kept reiterating to me. "Like unwanted grease sizzling in a frying pan; fuckin' wiped-out!"

Private Morgan attested and elaborated that he had hid under the dead horse for a long time, furtively peeping-out across the common for encroaching Martians on the prowl. The renowned First Cardigan Sweater Regiment soon arrived, and tried a frenzied rush designed to initiate a skirmish at the pit, but the unit's vain attempt was simply and easily thwarted, for the enemy, with facility, eradicated and swept the prestigious unit right out of earthly existence.

Then, according to Private Morgan's lucid recounting, the swiftly constructed metallic monster had risen to its feet, and had begun leisurely maneuvering left and right across the turfy common, savagely slaughtering the remaining fleeing, fugitive British troops. Its head-like hood was revolving about, exactly like the head and neck of a ventriloquist's manikin dummy. A kind of steel arm carried a complicated metallic case, about which green flashes scintillated, and out of the funnel of that awesome weapon, the dreadful black smoke and green beam shot-out of the extremely demonic, multi-functional Heat-Ray generator."

"Holy shit in High Heaven's toilets!" I boisterously exclaimed. "The fucked-up Martians won't even leave us unfortunate survivors a beggar's pot to pee in! Did the cavalry troops arrive on the battle scene and die like Jesus on Calvary?" I stupidly asked.

Private Henry Morgan then continued his fascinating narrative. "After a few minutes of unprecedented combat, not a breathing human or living thing was left upon the common, and just about every bush and tree growing upon the area were already blackened skeletons because of the excessive huge burnings. The elite cavalry horsemen had been arriving on the road beyond the pit's curvature," Morgan proceeded to detail. "And then the apocalyptic Heat-Ray was instantaneously implemented, and in a matter of seconds, the entire town of Woking became a heap of fiery ruins."

Next, the deadly Thing shut-off the lethal green ray, and turning its back upon me, the mobile structure smugly began waddling away towards the smoldering pine woods that coincidentally sheltered the second cylinder. As the newly-formed walking fort did so, another glittering Titan had, in minutes, almost-magically built itself up out of the original pit."

The second extraordinary monster followed the first in an improvised single file, and at that critical juncture, Private Morgan emphasized that he began crawling very cautiously across the hot heather ash towards Horsell. The young survivor managed to escape alive into the parallel ditch found by the side of the road, and so evaded the perfidious adversary's destructive green rays, with Henry's route heading toward Woking.

"Woking roads were virtually impassable with strewn rubble laying everywhere. It seemed that there were a few people still alive there, frantic for the most part, and many were severely burned and scalded," Private Morgan recalled and shared. "I turned aside and hid among some scorching heaps of broken wall, as one of the Martian metallic giants returned, presumably to perform some esoteric espionage, or perhaps engage in some kind of perverted, clandestine, strategic survey."

"What were the Martians surveying if the scurrilous dickheads already had destroyed nearly the entire Woking population, along with the majority of the town's buildings," I wondered and asked.

"What really made me especially nauseous was when I witnessed this one old man being stalked and pursued, looking much like a mouse being toyed-with and chased by a hungry stray cat. Finally, after satisfying its play, one of the machine's steely tentacles lifted the unfortunate fellow off the ground, and knocked the poor guy's head against the wide trunk of a tall pine tree. At last, after nightfall, I made a diligent rush and got over the railway embankment, and eventually, wandering around in a daze, I wound-up at your doorstep."

Then, disconsolate Private Henry Morgan began sobbing again, and in a brief minute, gathered enough energy to somberly relate that he had been skulking along towards Maybury Hill, in the hope of getting out of direct encroaching danger.

"I discovered people hiding in trenches and cellars," Morgan stressed, "and many of the survivors had made-off towards the hamlet of Send. Other neurotic residents threatened me to 'Get the hell out of here!' At last, after nightfall, I made a diligent rush to Maybury Hill, and luckily and safely, studying my area map, got over the railway embankment, and eventually, wandering around, I wound-up begging for food and shelter at your doorstep."

That was the descriptive story I had gotten from Private Henry Morgan, bit by bit. Eventually, towards the end, the young enlisted man became calmer and less demonstrative, telling me concise particulars, and trying to make me see the matters as he had experienced them.

Morgan had not eaten any substantial food rations since midday yesterday, as the famished soldier had informed me early in his narrative, and I found some fatty mutton and stale bread in the pantry. I brought the non-nutritious food into the kitchen, and my new acquaintance ate the edibles ravenously. We lit no lamp for fear of attracting the Martians wrath, and ever and again, our greedy hands would together touch upon the remaining paltry portions of bread and meat.

As Henry talked, secret topics discussed during our meeting came-out of the darkness, and the trampled flower plants and broken rose bushes, all quite probably caused by desperate, itinerant trespassers searching the garbage bin for edible scraps outside my window, became much more distinct and understandable. It would seem that a number of hungry men and starving animals had recently rushed across the lawn to the full trash bin. As my fatigued guest spoke, I began to closely scrutinize Private Morgan's youthful face, which was blackened and haggard, as no doubt mine was also.

When we had finished eating our not-so-scrumptious meal, Henry and I walked softly upstairs to the loft, and I looked again out of the room's window. In one wild night, the valley had become a meadow of glowing ashes. By then, the fires had somewhat dwindled. Where flames had been raging, there were no streams of smoke that had reached my home, which had formerly made Morgan and me choke incessantly.

But the countless ruins of shattered houses, the collapsed church, the mostly-demolished school down the lane, and now gaunt, decimated rural retail shops still were simmering in the pitiless light of late dawn.

Yet, here and there, some object had had the luck to escape the Martian onslaught. A white railway signal had survived at the Maybury Hill depot, and the skeleton frame of a greenhouse stood intact down the lane.

Never before in the history of warfare had destruction been so indiscriminate and so instantly devastating. And shining with the growing light emanating from the east, three of the metallic giants were roaming about the pit, their cowls rotating as though they were keenly assessing and analyzing the widespread desolation they had made.

It seemed to me that the sandpit had been enlarged, and ever and again, vivid puffs of green vapor streamed-up and out towards the brightening dawn.

Beyond were the pillars of fire encircling neighboring Chobham. Morgan then felt an urge to make a pertinent comment in the form of a question.

"What the hell do these evil Martians want?" the distraught army non-deserter asked. "They're Satan's revenge on mankind, yes, they are! The dirty bastards must have some secret Achilles heel somewhere!"

"That's easy to answer," I suavely replied. "The vile invaders want to take over our precious Earth, and wish to either enslave or kill all human life that previously had dominion over this targeted planet! You don't have to be Sherlock Holmes to figure *that* conundrum out! You don't even have to be Dr. Watson!"

"I regret that in the past, I had taken our planet for granted," Morgan sadly confessed. "But now, I realize exactly how fragile it, you, and me really are!"

Chapter 12

"DUAL DESTRUCTION"

As the dawn grew brighter, Private Henry Morgan and I withdrew from the window from which we had watched the Martians' maneuvers enacted upon the common, and together, my new friend and I very quietly stepped downstairs from the loft to review what we had just observed upstairs.

I had enjoyed commiserating with Henry, and by then, we both trusted each other's character. The artillery wagon driver agreed with me that the house was no place in which to permanently stay and hide. Private Morgan expressed that he would attempt making his way back to London, and rejoin his Number 12 battery of the acclaimed Horse Artillery.

My plan was to return at once to Leatherhead. The powers of the Martians had so greatly impressed me that I had resolved to hopefully find Beatrice, and then retreat to Newhaven, and next, travel with my wife out of the country, perhaps to the United States. For I already perceived clearly that the metropolitan London area would inevitably become the epicenter of a disastrous struggle, before creatures such as those scumbag Martians could ever be once and for all destroyed.

Between Maybury Hill and Leatherhead, however, lay the third pernicious cylinder, with its metallic, petulant giants. Had I been alone, I think I should have taken my chances and struck across country to Wales. But the artilleryman dissuaded me.

"It's no special kindness to the right sort of wife to make her into a sorrowing widow," Private Morgan ethically remarked. "I'm sure that your dear Beatrice had been a loyal wife who practiced fidelity, and she probably never read any sinful pornography magazines like many sex-crazed spouses often do."

Despite Henry's incorrect perception of Beatrice's bizarre sexual habits, in the end, I agreed to accompany him, under cover of the woods, northward at least as far as Cobham Street, before my new friend and I might part company. Thereafter, my intention was to make a big detour by Epsom to eventually reach Leatherhead.

I should have started-out at once, but my new-found associate had been in active service, and Henry knew better than to set-out while rescuers and military police was scurrying-about on lookout patrol. Morgan was very persuasive and convinced me to rummage through the house for a flask, which after found, my army guest filled with rye whiskey, which according to manipulative Henry, would serve as an essential liquid "for medicinal purposes only".

"Are you sure you're not an alcoholic?" I interrogated. "Come clean, now! You do like to chug, don't you?"

"Well, if you really want to know," Henry jested with a broad grin. "I'm not an avid drinker, but my cousins Tom Collins, Jim Beam, and Jack Daniels certainly are!"

"You belong in a deck of cards as one of the jokers," I quipped. "You're wild enough, and you do whatever pleasure suits you!"

"Okay, then, hot shot," Morgan retorted. "When we meet again in London, I'll buy you a shovel and a police nightstick, and give you a choice to either be the Ace of Spades or the Jack of Clubs!"

And as Henry and I carefully packed our food supplies, we lined every available pocket with packets of biscuits, and also, my remaining slices of rancid-smelling meat. Then, we stealthily crept-out of the chilly house, and scuttled as quickly as we could down the pot-holed road by which I had recently arrived overnight.

The cottages we trotted by seemed bleak and deserted. In the road lay a group of three charred bodies situated close together, apparently struck dead by some Martian secret weapon. And here and there were personal items that fleeing people had dropped: a clock, a slipper, a silver spoon, a dildo, a locket, and similar paraphernalia of sentimental value.

At the wide corner turning-up towards the village post office, a horseless cart, once filled with stacked boxes and furniture, had turned-over on a broken wheel, with its former cargo strewn all over the roadway. A cash box had been hastily smashed open and thrown near the debris, indicating that some prior larceny had probably taken place. But in actuality, nothing, not even money, meant anything to either the Martians or the panicky, escaping Maybury Hill residents.

Except for the administrative lodge at the Orphanage, which incidentally was still on fire, none of the adjacent houses had yet suffered extensive damage. The awesome Heat-Ray had shaved the chimney tops and had passed by to select and obliterate bigger and more impressive structures. Yet, besides ourselves, there did not seem to be a living soul evident anywhere on Maybury Hill.

"Where is everyone?" Morgan curiously asked. "Your village is now a veritable ghost town! And they've all abandoned their haunted houses that are now lacking spooky dead phantoms, ghastly ghouls, and gay goblins!"

"Take another swig of rye whiskey," I advised my traveling colleague. "You'll find plenty of spirits to inhabit your brain if you elect to chug-down the entire rye contents of our flask."

We furtively ambled further down the abandoned lane, where I showed Morgan the motionless body of the man in black, alias Mr. Cedrick Jones. Flies and disgusting crawling maggots were eating away at his already decaying flesh.

"We don't have time to bury him. We don't even have any shovel between us," Henry sadly related. "Your inn owner can't even make it to the wrong side of the grass."

'May Jones rest in peace!' I quietly prayed. "He was not a religious man, Henry, so I suppose that old Cedrick is now selling devils food cakes for that apostate Lucifer. And let perpetual light shine upon his fat ugly ass!"

Even the forest birds were hushed, and as we hurried along our desolate route that paralleled the woods, Morgan and I talked in low whispers, and our eyes nervously scanned our whereabouts now and again over our encumbered shoulders, putting-down our back packs. Once or twice, being worried, we stopped to listen for signs of unusual forest activity.

After a short time, we drew nearer the road, and as we did so, our ears heard the clatter of hoofs, and our pupils noticed through the hanging tree branches that three cavalry soldiers were riding slowly towards Woking. We hailed the horsemen, and the trio abruptly halted and drew their sabers, suspecting that Henry and I were road bandits or cutthroat robbers. My companion whispered to me that the horsemen were a lieutenant and a couple of privates, all members of the 8th Cavalry.

"You're the first men I've seen coming this way," declared the lieutenant. "What's brewing?"

"Not coffee, that's for damned sure!" I facetiously joked, not realizing that I could have been run through by the lieutenant's raised weapon.

The officer was eager to learn *our* singular identities as the two lower-ranked soldiers stared suspiciously at our noticeable, uncomfortable presence. Henry saved my tender ass from being swiftly executed by automatically saluting his new superior officer.

"The large gun I was conveying had destroyed my artillery wagon last night, Sir. I've been hiding since then with this intrepid gentleman," Henry disclosed. "I'm trying to rejoin my battery, Sir. You'll soon come in sight of the Martians, I expect, about a mile along this road. Beware of their destructive Heat-Ray! It's already killed hundreds of soldiers and fine citizens."

"What the dickens are these invading Martians like?" asked the lieutenant.

"They certainly aren't like Charles Dickens!" I jested.

Again, Private Henry Morgan rescued my ass. "They operate metallic giants in thick armor, Sir. The villains use these incredible huge killing machines that are a hundred feet high," Henry continued answering. "Three legs attached onto each colossal machine, all of them having a separate metallic body, something like aluminum, I believe. And the mobile forts each possess a mighty head concealed inside a hood, which protects the mechanism from being attacked, Sir. The Martians and their machines certainly are not nondescript! That Sir, is about all I can relate!"

"Get out! Are you sane?" replied the lieutenant. "What confounded nonsense! Have you been fucked-up ever since you've been conceived in your mother's womb? Are you on drugs, or perhaps you're just basically mentally retarded. Say, I believe I smell rye whiskey!"

"You'll soon see for yourself, Sir," Henry smartly elaborated. "The Martians carry a kind of box, Sir, that shoots fire and green rays that strike dead and disintegrate any soldiers impeding their path."

"What do ya' mean by a gun? The Winchesters that are used to guard the altar at Winchester Cathedral? Ha, ha, ha!"

"No, Sir," Henry all-too-courteously replied. "Their deadly Heat-Ray is undoubtedly a hundred times more powerful, and much more devastating, than our most advanced cannons. A dozen of those Martian machines could easily obliterate downtown London in less than half an hour!"

The lieutenant looked at me and asked, "Is this bullshit that he's jabbering accurate? I advise that your companion not instill panic among the public. If he continues to spread fear, then your son-of-a-bitchin' pal might be eligible for a swift court martial!"

"It's perfectly true," I confirmed, without being a venerable bishop or a qualified priest. "I'll swear by it on a stack of crucifixes! The Martians are octopus-like reptiles with long, dangling tentacles. I suspect that the aliens might possibly be carnivorous flesh addicts, who reportedly randomly devour humans. I don't know about the cannibal bullshit aspect, but I do know that the unpredictable sons-of-bitches have amphibian, snake-like, anatomical features!"

"Well," snorted and smiled the army lieutenant. "I suppose it's my business to move ahead and see for myself the side-show freaks, too. I don't know what the hell you're smoking, Stranger, but I wish I had a pound of it to enjoy."

Then, the no-nonsense lieutenant switched from berating me to speaking directly to Private Morgan. Look here," the formal officer imperatively addressed Henry. "We're detailed to patrol this area and assigned the task of clearing people out of their houses. You'd better go along and report yourself to Brigadier-General Marvin, and tell him all you know. He's hunkered-down over at Weybridge. Know the way there?"

"I do," I verified, pretending to be getting married again. "I do! I live in this area! The private is from London and is unfamiliar with the terrain!" my vocal cords persuasively reiterated.

"A mile south of here, you say?" the lieutenant asked.

"At most," I answered, and pointed southward toward the distant treetops. "Be careful on your approach!"

The officer thanked me for the pertinent information and rode on with his small contingent, and Henry and I never again saw the three army soldiers.

Further along our difficult hike, Morgan and I came upon a group of three women and two children being active by the roadside, apparently busy clearing-out a laborer's cottage. The stranded stragglers, evidently lowlife peasants pilfering readily available items, had "borrowed" a small hand truck, and were piling-up the dolly with bundles of unclean clothes and shabby furniture. The five scruffy-looking tramps were all too assiduously engaged in their purloining activity, so Private Morgan let them be, since law and order had already disintegrated into anarchy.

By Byfleet Station, we emerged from the dark pine trees, and found the country road calm and peaceful under the morning sunlight. We were far beyond the range of the potent Heat-Ray, and had it not been for the silent robberies occurring in some of the houses, along with the stirring movement of residents' emergency packing legally going-on inside others, and the knot of soldiers standing upon the stone bridge over the railway tracks, staring-down the line towards Woking, the day would have seemed very like any normal Sunday.

"Say, Henry," I diplomatically articulated. "I've told you all about my wife, Beatrice. I assume you aren't married, and that you're relatively manly, and not a wimpy member of the LBGTQRSTUVW community. But truthfully; do you have a special woman, a sweetheart in your life?"

"Why, yes," Morgan declared with a rare broad grin showing upon his lips. "In fact, the Martians and this here marsh remind me of my fondest girlfriend Marsha, who loves eating marshmallows! But tell me, something, Herbert. How did you meet Beatrice, and what attracted you to her?"

"Well, Henry; let's just say that I found my thrill, on Maybury Hill, and leave it at that!"

Several squeaky-wheeled horse-drawn farm wagons and smaller private carts were moving creakily along the road toward Addlestone, and suddenly through the gate of a grower's field, Morgan and I saw, across a stretch of flat meadow, six twelve-pounders standing neatly at equal distances, all pointing towards Woking.

The assigned soldiers stood by their respective blasters, impatiently waiting for instructions to fire, and the ammunition supply wagons were positioned behind in a semi-circle, at a business-like distance. The servicemen stood at strict attention, almost as if they were undergoing an inspection inside their barracks.

"That's good!" I remarked to Henry. "They'll get one fair shot, at any rate, but I regret that's all they'll have before being incinerated."

"I believe that the mortuary schools could learn plenty from the Martians in terms of performing quick cremations," Morgan pessimistically commented. "As the Holy Bible says; ashes to ashes; dust to dust!"

Further on towards Weybridge, just over the old stone span, there were a number of men in white fatigue jackets throwing up a long rampart, and more large guns had been strategically stationed behind.

"It's bows and arrows against the lightning-like green rays, anyhow," claimed Henry. "The naïve troops over there haven't seen the likes of that wicked fire-beam yet. God bless them!"

"That's one time they wouldn't want to be on the beam," I returned in a not-too-frequent jovial disposition. "Those poor blokes will soon be sacrilegiously reduced to embers, cinders, and dust particles. Not even the Pope and the Archbishop of Canterbury are sufficiently safe from the fucked-up Heat-Ray!"

The officers, who were not actively engaged in the physical labor, stood in a straight line, and their eyes stared over the treetops looking southwestward, as their toiling subordinates were aggressively digging defensive trenches and bunkers. The lower-rank soldiers would stop their excavations every now and again to fearfully peer in the same direction toward Maybury Hill.

Byfleet was in an absolute tumult; townspeople were feverishly packing suitcases and boxes, and a score of elite hussars, some of them being dismounted from their steeds, others still on horseback, were gossiping about the looming Martian threat in random groups. Three or four black government wagons, with crosses neatly painted in white circles, and an old and tarnished omnibus, were being loaded with newly arrived munitions and food supplies in the village square.

The soldiers, many of them short-tempered, were having the greatest difficulty in making the uninformed rowhouse dwellers realize the gravity of their impending dilemma. Henry and I saw one shriveled old fellow with a huge box and a score of flower pots containing beautiful orchids, angrily expostulating with the on-duty corporal, who was advising the old codger to leave the exotic flowers behind in order to facilitate a more orderly evacuation. I abruptly stopped and gripped the street vendor's wrinkle-skinned arm to alert the geezer of the imminent danger.

"Do you know what's over there?" I hollered above all the rowdy disorganization around us, while pointing at the pine tops that remarkably camouflaged the invincible Martian monstrosities on the move.

"Eh?" said the elderly hawker, turning toward my frowning face. "I wish to sell my expensive orchids. Leave me the fuck alone!"

"Do I look like a blooming idiot!" I vehemently ranted to the flower merchant. "Death is stalking your ass!" I shouted. "Death is coming! Death! Do you hear?" I repeated in a loud tone of frustration.

And leaving the obstinate, hoary asshole alone to process what I had described, I hurried ahead to reunite with Morgan's rapid cadence. At the main intersection's waterfront corner, I looked back and viewed the stubborn lowlife street peddler still standing by his display box, with the gorgeous orchids arranged upon its planked lid, and the old gent's squinting eyes were staring vaguely over the towering trees as if he were waiting for a divine miracle to pay him a personal visit.

No one in Weybridge could tell either Henry or me where the makeshift military headquarters had recently been established. The whole place was in such frenzied confusion, of which I had never before observed in any rural town. Carts, wagons, and carriages were in disarray everywhere, with those vehicles clogging every major traffic artery. The respectable inhabitants of the place, men attired in golf and boating costumes, and their spoiled wives, prettily dressed in alluring gowns, were hectically packing their valuables, and also, hired drunken riverside loafers were energetically helping to expedite the requested chores.

Town children were both amused and excited at the unusual tumult, and the youngsters were highly-delighted that they were avoiding the monotony of the traditional Sunday church service. In the midst of it all, the appalled local vicar was extremely disappointed at the Sunday departure from normal attendance regularity, and the upset preacher was futilely ringing his clanging bell for his preoccupied congregation to enter his empty place of worship.

Henry and I remained at Weybridge until midday, and at that noon hour we found ourselves at the park near Shepperton Lock, precisely near where the Wey and the Thames had their confluence. Part of the time we spent helping two old women pack a little cart with boxes of sanitary napkins, flimsy bras, silk panties, and used girdles that the pair had been selling.

The Wey River had a small marina where tourist boats were being hired to transport residents across the river to Shepperton, and anxious crowds were gathering in prolific numbers to make the assumed excursion to what the shouting people presently considered a much safer harbor town.

As yet, the flight to safety had not grown into a wild panic, but there were already far more desperate people waiting than all the boats navigating passengers across the Wey could accommodate. Families came panting along, suffering under the heavy burden of carrying loaded trunks; one husband and wife duo were even carrying a detached outhouse door, with some of their household goods piled upon it.

Across the Thames, except where the transit boats were landing and unloading, everything was relatively quiet, in vivid contrast with the more active Surrey side. The ferry passengers who had landed on the Shepperton dock went tramping-off down the lane, seeking food and hotel lodging. The big ferryboat had just made a profitable journey, and its lower and upper decks appeared to be full to capacity.

Four soldiers stood upon the lawn of the Shepperton Inn on the opposite side of the river, staring and jesting at the frantic fugitives, without ever offering to render assistance. The inn had been closed for much-needed renovations, and so, the new arrivals were asking residents on the Thames side if any rooms were available to rent at any price. Soon, a busy black market was thriving in Shepperton.

"What's that boom?" cried an alarmed boatman.

"Shut up, you irritating fool!" yelled a man to his yelping dog, whose acute hearing had first perceived the distant gunfire. Then the sound came again, but a trifle louder; this time coming from the direction of Chertsey, a muffled-but-distinct thud.

A woman screamed like a banshee as the military defenses commenced initiating their futile cannon blasts. Everyone stood, all ears arrested by the sudden stir of a developing battle. Tranquility and British hospitality had, in a minute, transformed into chaos and anarchy.

"The soldiers will surely stop the little green men," a rather nervous woman maintained. "How could an army of leprechauns beat our well-trained British troops?"

Then suddenly, everyone facing north visually discerned a rush of smoke billowing skyward up near the river bend, and thereafter, the ground trembled under foot as a heavy explosion shook the air several hundred feet away, with the blast smashing windows of the houses on both sides of the Wey, and leaving all spectators astonished and petrified.

"Here they are!" shouted a man in a blue jersey who was not from Jersey. "Over yonder! Do you see the bastards approaching? Turn your smelly asses around and look yonder!"

Quickly and surprisingly, one after the other, three of the tall, armored, mobile forts appeared, and soon were easily visible over the line of pine trees, and the machines were moving in synchronized precision across the flat meadows that stretched towards Chertsey. Diminutive, cowled figures, the encroaching hulks seemed at first, advancing in lockstep, a half-mile away, with a rolling motion that intimidated us all.

"Three appears to be their lucky number!" Henry yelled to me above the numerous explosions and detonations. "Everything the Martians do seem to aptly revolve around the number three! I wonder if the fucked-up lizard bastards and snake bitches have reproductive sex in threesomes!"

Henry and I were in a tight knit of crazed folks waiting for the next ferry to sail across the Wey. Our eavesdropping ears were privy to a weird in-progress conversation between an unnerved husband and his distressed wife.

"I'll tell ya', Mabel. Those lucky Hawaiians and Texans have a big advantage over we English folk."

"Why's that William?"

"Because the Hawaiians can kill the freakin' Martians by shoving prickly pineapples up their posteriors, and the courageous Texans could do likewise by forcing those thorny desert cactus plants up aliens' assholes in a similar manner."

Another conversation was overheard above the public commotion as Henry and I were eavesdropping on a discussion between two agitated local hookers, who were evaluating a possible loss of business.

"Listen, Daisy. We're gonna' have to either find a new profession, or be reeducated quickly."

"How come, Dottie?"

"Because how the hell are we gonna' have quality sex with goddamned lizards, snakes and non-paying octopuses," Daisy vociferously argued. "Those bastard Martians are ruinin' our careers, and those invading lizard freaks that are trapped inside that pit over near Maybury Hill, well, I think that those rotten shitheads don't know their ass from a lousy hole in the ground."

Then, advancing obliquely towards us came a fourth, fifth and sixth Martian machine, which all were detectable advancing and emitting the oddball words, "Atoo! Atoo! Atoo!" Their armored exteriors glittered in the sunlight as the fantastic juggernauts swept swiftly forward upon the army's sterile guns and ineffective cannon fire. Quite predictably, a ghostly, terrible Heat-Ray had been aimed toward Chertsey, and the ray struck the town like an enormous, errant lightning bolt.

At the sight of those strange, swift, and terrible Martian war devices, the crowd standing near the water's edge seemed to become momentarily horror-struck. There was no screaming or shouting, but simply a shocked and disbelieving silence.

Unexpectedly, a toothless old woman with a hoarse voice thrust forward behind me, and nearly dislodged my dangling testicles. I turned and joined the rush of the hysterical mob, who finally fully comprehended that the Martian weapons could easily reduce their bodies to ashes, thus sending their sinful souls soaring into the hereafter. The terrible Heat-Ray was dominant and foremost in my beleaguered mind, and I screamed to petrified Henry, "Get under water!"

Morgan and I dove into the river, and pretending to be accomplished mallards, quickly ducked our heads under the cold current. Others mimicked our stellar example and duplicated our impulsive behavior.

Then, as the Martian menace towered overhead, scarcely a hundred-yards away, I again flung myself forward under the river's surface. The splashes of the people leaping into the water from inside the crossing boats sounded like thunderclaps to my submerged ears.

The Martian navigator, presumably operating the first tall machine, took no more notice, since the fiends seemed more interested in slaughtering large numbers of fleeing humans rather than individuals, one by one. When I became half-drowned, I raised my head above the surface, and my eyes soon learned that the invaders' formidable hood was directly pointing at the army batteries that were still firing useless shells across the river. The muddy banks were seemingly cluttered with delirious people that had leaped into the river from the ferry, and then had waded ashore.

In another moment, the Martian apparatus had become positioned above the left bank, and in a stride, was wading halfway across the channel. The knee hinges of its legs bent at the farther bank, and in another moment, the mobile fort had raised itself to its full height again, close to the village of Shepperton.

Then, I heard and saw six hidden army cannons firing simultaneously. The sudden concussions were occurring near my location at the river's edge, and my heart began pounding and pulsating. The mammoth steel monster was already raising the specialized casement that had been generating the horrendous Heat-Ray, when the first fired army shell missed its mark and burst six-yards above the hood.

I gave a cry of astonishment, as I thought nothing of the other two nearby lethal Martian monsters on patrol; my distracted attention was next riveted upon the nearer incident. Without hesitation, two other shells burst in the air next to the shiny machine's body, as the hood twisted around in time to receive the direct impact, but not in time to dodge the more accurate fourth shell, which burst clean in the face of the 'Kill Thing'. The hood bulged, flashed, and was whirled-off in a dozen tattered fragments of grey flesh and glittering metal.

"Hit!" I shouted, with an exclamation vacillating somewhere between a scream and a cheer. Then, I noticed Henry surfacing from his most recent dive, and feeling temporary exultation, I gleefully shrieked in his direction, since I became euphoric at seeing that my army friend was still alive and lustily breathing.

The decapitated alien colossus reeled like a drunken giant; but to my consternation, the gargantuan hulk did not fall over. Instead, it almost miraculously recovered its balance, and, amazingly and inexplicably, actually began repairing itself.

However, despite its desperate attempt at rejuvenation, the alien war machine erratically marched along in a crooked path, incapable of employing regular guidance and control. Its swinging right arm struck the tower of the Shepperton Anglican Church, smashing the steeple down to the street below. And finally, the injured mobile fort blundered on and collapsed with tremendous force, and the crash made a prodigious splash into the Wey.

"The alien assholes are indeed vulnerable after all!" I exuberantly exclaimed to Morgan. "The fuckheads can be defeated!" I triumphantly yelled.

"Sort of," Henry answered. "But the damned ratio will be a hundred army units to one Martian machine!"

Right after our short dialogue had terminated, another violent explosion shook the air, and a spout of water, steam, mud, and shattered metal shot far up into the sky. As the fearful roving "Heat-Ray camera" splashed into the shallow river, the sensor flashed into a cloud of steam. In another moment, a huge wave, like a mud-laden tidal tsunami, but actually scalding hot, came sweeping around the bend upstream.

Henry and I rapidly clambered back onto the nearby bank, but at least a hundred screaming and shouting novice swimmers were being scalded by the oncoming boiling killer wave, and the frantic recipients were doomed to perish.

Thick clouds of steam were pouring-off the downed-enemy fort's wreckage, and through the tumultuously whirling wisps, quite intermittently and vaguely, the contraptions' gigantic limbs had been wildly churning the water, and flinging and spraying quantities of hot mud and sand into the air in all directions.

The Thing's grotesque tentacles swayed and struck everything in sight like fabled sea serpent arms, and, save for the helpless purposelessness of these shifting movements, the misadventure was as if some massive, wounded, berserk, mythological sea creature was struggling for its life amid the rippling waves. Enormous quantities of a ruddy-brown fluid, presumably oil, were spurting-up in noisy jets out of the disabled monster.

"The son-of-a-bitch seems to be ejaculating a volley of orgasms," Henry indulgently screamed, and then wiped the remaining water from his brow. "Chalk one up for the British side."

"The metallic bastard finally got into the swim of things," I replied like a starving comedian entertaining a small audience at the wholly dishonorable Woking Gay and Lesbian Burlesque Theater.

My attempt at amateur humor was soon diverted from that death flurry by a furious nearby yelling, a sound like that of a high-pitched siren used in our manufacturing cities, such as London and Manchester. A man, knee-deep in mud next to the towing path, shouted inaudibly to me while pointing upward.

Looking back, my eyes noticed the other Martian behemoths advancing in gigantic strides down the riverbank from the direction of Chertsey. However, the Shepperton guns had been efficiently neutralized and silenced by the superior enemy weaponry.

For a moment, I raised my head to take a deep breath and scrape the hair and water from my eyes. The irritating steam was rising in a whirling white fog, that at first, altogether hid the Martians from my view. The surrounding noise was deafening. Then, I again saw the enemy units. Dim, noisy, colossal figures of grey, their forms magnified by the hot mist. The towering "kill machines" had passed by me, and the two units were currently stooping-over the frothing, tumultuous ruins of their disjointed comrade.

The third and fourth "kill machines" stood beside their fallen comrade partially lying in the shallow water, one of them perhaps two-hundred-yards from me, and the other towering behemoth facing towards Laleham. The generators of the Heat-Ray's engine revved higher, and the hissing green beams smote-down this way and that, seemingly in the act of dying.

The air was full of ear-shattering sounds, amply defining a deafening and confusing conflict of competing noises. The clangorous din of the Martians' advance; the crash of falling houses and commercial buildings; the nerve-racking thud of trees, fences, and sheds flashing into flame, along with the crackling and roaring of various nearby infernos triggered supreme horror among all terrified eyewitnesses.

Dense black smoke had been frightfully leaping-up to mingle with the hot steam that was still ascending from the river, and as the moss-green Heat-Ray redundantly waved to-and-fro over Weybridge, its selected targets blazed with fresh flashes of incandescent white, that instantaneously gave place to smoky, lurid flames. The nearer houses still stood intact, awaiting their ultimate fate, appearing shadowy, faint and ash-covered in the enveloping steam, with the fires behind them going amok in all directions.

For a moment, perhaps, I stood there, dumbfounded and dazed in a semi-trance, my sagging spirit feeling hopeless of escape from the ongoing living hell. Through the encompassing reek, I could see the many people who had been with me and Morgan, splashing and thrashing in the river; and then scrambling-out of the water through the high reeds, like little frogs hurrying through high grass to escape the hunger of an awaiting predator in search of a meal.

Then suddenly, the white and green intimidating flashes of the Heat-Ray came leaping towards Henry and me. The idyllic houses on the waterfront street caved-in as the roofs and frames dissolved at the green beam's malignant touch, and the attendant explosions darted-out furious flames. Next, I observed that the short, planted trees in the lane had changed into intense fires, all erupting into a lengthy, spectacular roar.

The phantom Death-Ray flickered-up and down the towing path, easily annihilating the targeted people who were zig-zagging this way and that, and the satanic device blasted everything in sight, executing its tormenting evil only fifty-yards from where I stood.

The "Death Beam" swept across the vaporous river over to Shepperton, and the water between the river's banks rose in a twirling spiral, and soon mystically crested in a display of boiling-hot steam.

The very huge, newly-generated, heat-wave had unexpectedly rushed upon me, right where I had again been standing in the shallow water. I screamed aloud, being badly scalded on my exposed hands and arms, and momentarily, also being half-blinded.

And in an agonized condition, my weak legs staggered through the hissing water with me heading towards the sandy Shepperton shore. Had my foot stumbled, it would have definitely been my bitter end.

I fell to the ground, helpless, and in full sight of the Martians. My body came to rest upon the broad, bare, gravelly spit that runs down to mark the angle of where the Wey joins the Thames. Fearing my demise, my exhausted mind anticipated nothing but certain death. I glanced around, totally exhausted, but there was no sign of Private Morgan. All that my half-blinded eyes could detect were random heaps of ashes.

Chapter 13

"HIDING WITH THE CURATE"

The Martian attack enacted at the confluence of the Wey and the Thames rivers corresponded to the last I had ever seen of Army Private Henry Morgan. I thoroughly searched the area around the bulkhead, bur Morgan was nowhere to be found. My only hope was that the dreaded Heat-Ray had not taken his life, and that dear Henry would eventually be able to reunite with his army unit in London. Regardless, friends come into one's life and suddenly leave, as if you and they are occasional customers entering and exiting a London department store's revolving door.

My befuddled mind got to thinking about the human race's brief tenure upon this unique Earth, which has been here for an estimated four or five billion years. In a short span, our industrious ancestors had achieved a most meritorious evolution and development.

A mere hundred-thousand-years ago in eternal time, our primitive species had been a collection of random hunters living in dank caves and wobbly huts. Neanderthals and Cro-Magnons might have eventually discovered how to make fire, which naturally attracted animals to their archaic campfires. Over time, primitive men and women learned the basic rudiments of civilization, which occurred right after the domestication of animals. Roaming clans had settled into communities when meat could be obtained from butchering domesticated and herded sheep, goats and cows, and soon thereafter, the secret of the seed had been discovered, and vegetable and fruit crops could then be sowed and harvested.

Around a mere four-thousand-years ago, the Egyptian, the Mesopotamian and the Greek empires were being established, and later, around 1000 BC, alphabets and writing were invented, and that is really when cultures and human creativity came into worldwide prominence.

During the reign of the Roman Emperor Nero, who played his fiddle while his city burned, marked the beginning of the decline of organized law and order. In the five-hundreds A.D., Vandals and other barbarian tribes devastated the remnants of classical Rome, and the western world had been egregiously thrust into a wasted period known as the Dark Ages.

But around 1,000 A.D., the marvelous Renaissance began; and invention and culture were admirably resurrected, where great works of art and imagination by such sage geniuses as Michelangelo and Leonardo Da Vinci brought civilization back to life, and wealthy Italy ascended to new cultural heights, culminating with inspired Galileo inventing the first functional telescope.

Then next came the Protestant Reformation, where independent Christian religions brought about new-found freedoms of thought, and *that* philosophical rebellion against the authoritarian Catholic Church gradually led to the Age of Exploration and the Age of Scientific Discovery, spearheaded by sagacious Sir Isaac Newton. And thereafter, the ensuing Age of Reason, led by British John Locke and the Frenchman Voltaire, eventually gave birth to the United States Declaration of Independence and Constitution, which extended basic ideas that had been founded in the landmark Magna Carta, signed by King John of England, back in the 1300s, which was the first significant step toward democracy against tyrannical dukes and kings.

The Age of Reason also contributed to the genesis of the great Industrial Revolution of the 1800s, where factories manufactured products and commodities, which created the burgeoning middle-class societies in England, Germany, and America. Inventions such as trains and railroad systems improved transportation and mobility among appreciative, thriving populations.

And now, with this terrible intrusion into our planet's short cultural and scientific history by the barbaric Martians, heartless fiends possessing advanced military technology, these strange and alien creatures from the red planet intend to destroy the evolving human progress that has admirably matured over the past five thousand years.

Their giant machines that utilize green Heat-Rays, and also fire-shooting electric White Disintegration Beams, which simulate the destructive powers of atmospheric lightning, will certainly propel the human race into extinction. Who would ever have hypothesized that intelligent reptilians, with snake-like and octopus physical characteristics, would successfully invade our blessed Earth and threaten to defeat and conquer all of human civilization in an unprecedented and crucial War of the Worlds?

After the Martians had received a sudden lesson in the power of British terrestrial weapons as demonstrated with the disabling of their mobile fort device near Shepperton, the very surprised Martians decided to retreat to their original position upon Horsell Common. And in their worried haste, and encumbered with the debris of their smashed Heat-Ray unit, the prowling bastards no doubt overlooked hunting-down a negligible victim such as myself at the Shepperton docks.

Had the ignorant fucks left their fallen comrade on the battlefield and intelligently pushed on to the north, there was nothing at that time resisting their advance between Weybridge and London, except perhaps a few disheveled batteries of twelve-pounder guns.

But indeed, the circus-side-show, reptilian freaks commanding the arcane cylinders were in no special hurry to proceed forward. Perhaps their leadership had been apprehensive about being inflicted additional casualties, or maybe the alien commanders were prudently waiting for hundreds of additional warships to arrive from Mars.

And meanwhile, the British military and naval authorities, now fully aware of the tremendous power of their heinous interplanetary antagonists, worked with furious energy to vigorously counteract the bellicose, reptilian fuckheads. Every ten minutes, a fresh gun came into a nearby position until, before twilight, every suburban villa on the hilly slopes about Kingston masked an expectant black muzzle.

And throughout the charred and desolate area, perhaps twenty square miles altogether that encircled the Martian encampment on

Horsell Common, inside the many ruined villages, crawled the devoted army scouts with their heliographs, which would warn entrenched gunners of the next Martian approach.

But the wily invaders now understood our command of (according to *their* standards) our obsolete artillery, and also of the danger of *our* military proximity, and not a brave soldier ventured within a mile of any mobile "killing machine", had the foolish intention of harassing or antagonizing the presently inactive enemy.

And while the temporarily stymied Martians behind me were scrupulously preparing for their next sally, I found some solace in realizing that in front of me, organized British battalions were gathering for the next decisive battle. With those vivid understandings in mind, I made my way with infinite pain, and exerted labor, from the fire and smoke of burning Weybridge, hobbling my way towards metropolitan London.

I saw an abandoned boat, very small and remote, drifting down-stream; and throwing-off most of my drenched and grimy clothes, I gained access to the dingey, and so escaped out of that devastated area of ugly destruction. There were no oars inside the skiff, but I contrived to paddle, as well as my swollen hands would allow, moving with extreme caution in a tedious effort down the narrow stream towards Halliford.

'I wonder if the Martians have sailing ships and if the shitheads can swim,' I mused. 'Of course, the feckless assholes can swim, if the dipshits are part octopus and part reptile or amphibian. And if they're also part snake as believed by the testimonies of reliable eyewitnesses, I hope that those alien snakes are yellow-bellied!'

The hot steamy water from the incredible Martian Heat-Ray application had flowed downstream with me, so that for the better part of a mile, I could see little of either bank. Once, however, my vision made-out a string of black figures hurrying and scurrying across the meadows from the direction of Weybridge. To my knowledge, Halliford, it seemed, had become deserted, and several of the houses facing the river were ablaze.

It was rather strange to see the distant town quite tranquil and deserted under the hot blue sky, with contaminating smoke and little threads of flame shooting straight-up into the heat of the afternoon. Never before had I seen houses burning without the accompaniment of an obstructive crowd, commonly known in central London as 'interfering dumb-shit ambulance-chasers'.

For a long time, I slowly drifted ahead with the stream's favorable current, feeling painful and weary after the terrifying perpetual violence I had been through, especially the intense steam-heat I had experienced upon and under the river back at Shepperton. Then, my mounting fears again got the better of me, and I resumed my redundant paddling.

At last, as a narrow bridge was coming into sight around the bend, my fever and faintness overcame my fears, and I landed on the Middlesex bank and lay down, musing in my perverted mind what the hell a 'middle sex' would look like, either on Earth or on Mars.

I suppose the time was then about four or five o'clock in the afternoon. My searching found a convenient area where I could pull the small boat onto land, hide it with brush and tree branches, and then I stumbled my way, perhaps half a mile, without confronting a human soul.

Then, feeling a lack of energy to proceed further, I laid-down in the shadow of a high hedge. My parched throat was very thirsty, and my harried mind was bitterly regretful that I had not earlier imbibed more water.

It is a curious thing, while I had been trudging along, that I felt anger at remembering my lost Beatrice. I cannot account for it, but my strong desire to eventually reach Leatherhead, to discover her safe and sound, gnawed at my conscience, and worried me excessively.

I do not clearly remember the arrival of the curate, so probably, I had been dozing upon his furtive approach. My mind became aware of his obese presence as my blinking eyes detected a seated figure in soot-smudged shirt sleeves, and I perceived that his upturned, clean-shaven face was staring at a faint, flickering campfire that the cleric had ignited.

The sky that time of year was what is called around southern England 'a mackerel', reflecting rows and rows of faint clouds, just tinted with the seasonal sunset. So therefore, at the sight of the fat curate in my midst, I naturally thought 'Holy Mackerel!'

I sat-up, and at the rustle of my motion, the fat-ass fellow looked at me quickly. "Have you any water?" I abruptly asked. "And I don't want to drink any damned Holy Water after hundreds of scummy fingers have dipped into it!"

The wannabe' minister negatively shook his head back and forth. "You've been asking for water in your deep sleep for the last hour," the charlatan padre stated. "That's all your out-of-sorts mind was thinking about. Do you have water on the brain?"

"Don't be ridiculous with your absurd comedy night routine," I admonished while feeling embarrassed, "or I might wildly chuck your corpulent ass into yonder stream to see if you'll either float or sink!"

'You're delusional because you've gone through hell already without even dying," the melancholy curate philosophically commented. "Your insufferable anguish has already-purged sin from your mortal soul without ever needing the fires of Satan's volcanic realm."

"Stop breaking my tenderloin balls," I obstinately answered. "I should immediately report your arrogant ass to the eminent Archbishop of Canterbury. His phone number is Et Cum Spiri: Tu Tuo."

For a brief moment we remained silent, taking further stock of each other. I dare say that the junior minister found me a strange enough figure, stripped-down, mostly naked, save for my water-soaked trousers, shoes and socks. My face and arms were coated with soot, and my shoulders were blackened by smudged smoke.

The curate's face was chubby; his chin short; his jaws seemingly retreated into his wrinkly neck, and his diminished hair lay in a twisted crisp, showing almost flaxen curls on his low forehead. The gent's eyes were rather large, pale blue, and blankly staring, something like a deer's pupils when reflected in the moonlight.

The white-collared church assistant spoke erratically and rapidly, with his beady eyes looking vacantly away from me as if he were ashamed to elucidate extensively about the odious Martian invasion.

"What does it mean?" the *alienated* fat slob asked. "What do these crazy things mean?"

I stared at him for a moment and made no definitive answer. "It means that your earthly religion doesn't mean an ounce of shit to the barbaric aliens."

The curate extended a plump white hand and spoke in almost a complaining tone of voice. "Why are these terrible things permitted? What wicked sins have we committed? The morning service was over, and I was walking through the peaceful roads to clear my cluttered brain in the early afternoon, and then, suddenly, fire, earthquake, death! It was as if it were Sodom and Gomorrah revisited! All our wonderful religious work has been undone; all the generous giving and good deeds unraveled! What are these insidious Martians up to?" the distraught asshole grieved, questioning his own value system. "Christ had died on the cross for what? For these ruthless savages from outer space?"

"About the terrible invasion," I interrupted and challenged. "You're a fuckin' *curate;* so why the hell can't you *cure it?"*

"Be kind to me, Sir," the flustered clergyman pleaded. "You sound like one of the cynical congregation members over in Leatherhead. Everyone there calls the toxic apostate Doubting Thomas, who incidentally is part owner of a lucrative soccer ball manufacturing company that earns a large *net* profit. If the obnoxious jerk wasn't such a benevolent contributor to the church treasury, I'd recommend that the archbishop swiftly and expeditiously excommunicate the sardonic troublemaker."

"It sounds like you, besides being a man of the cloth, you're also an avaricious man of the silk!" I vehemently retorted, looking at and assessing his corpulent paunch that appeared to be very well-fed.

The church assistant relapsed into silence, with his chin now sunken almost into his esophagus. Presently, the fanatical mental case began waving his hand, searching for elusive explanations to explain the vile Martian incursion into his former easy and simple life.

"All the bloody goodwill work has been eviscerated; along with all the benevolent Sunday school lessons. What have we done to deserve this evil scourge? What has Weybridge or Woking done? Everything that was worth building and keeping is gone; everything destroyed. The church! We rebuilt it only three years ago. Gone! Swept out of existence! Why?"

"You sound a lot like that frugal, gay faggot preacher over in Croydon, Parson Monius, I believe, is his name. The London tabloids reported that the notorious predator pedophile had started-out as a devout rector, who gladly took too many stiff salamis up the rectum!"

Another lengthy pause occurred following my curt depiction, and ignoring my acerbic rhetoric, the curate's words broke-out again, with his general elucidation sounding much like it had been originating from a demented psycho ward patient.

"The smoke of the sacred church's magnificent chimney; the edifice's splendid architecture, all going-up in flames!" the quixotic, asylum-bound ignoramus shouted in my face. "Why would the Almighty allow His own blessed altar to be so barbarically traduced and violated?"

The curate's tearful eyes flamed, and the ultra-religious nutcase pointed a lean finger in the direction of Weybridge. "My whole career has been wrecked because of these Martian atheists! My church and my rectum, er, I mean rectory, plundered because of bloodthirsty savages who know nothing about Jesus Christ dying on the cross for *their* many sins, nor do the interplanetary Vandals care one iota about their myriad destructive transgressions!"

By that very conflictive time, I was beginning to take the curate's mental depression full measure. The tremendous tragedy in which he had been involved, was glaringly evident in his distraught demeanor, with him being a helpless fugitive from Weybridge. I then fathomed how those circumstances had driven the disillusioned fool to the very edge of insanity.

"Are we far from Sunbury?" I asked in a rather matter-of-fact tone, just to articulate anything to change the subject from the vile Martian conquest to a calmer and more mundane topic.

"What are we to do?" the crazed imbecile asked. "Are these lecherous, salacious vipers everywhere? Has the Earth already been given over to accommodate these scurrilous predators?"

"Are we far from Sunbury?" I politely repeated. "We should be near."

"Only this morning, I officiated at early celebration, an ordinary Baptism. And now, the brazen Martians are initiating their own corrupt Baptism of Fire and Brimstone," the obsessed clergyman ranted like a raving maniac. "Brazen Martians!" I now say.

"Things have drastically changed," I quietly admitted. "You must keep your head out of your ass. According to your religious faith, there is still time for redemption. Start practicing what the fuck you believe in!"

"Bullshit, if not chickenshit!" the agitated curate stormily exclaimed. "This must be the beginning of the end," the nutjob impulsively insisted. "The end, I maintain! Perhaps it's heralding-in the Savior's vindictive Second Coming. Yes, that's it exactly! The great and terrible day of the Lord! Yes, Judgment Day; the Day of Reckoning! When men shall call upon the mountains and the rocks to fall upon them and hide their sins, and attempt concealing their true identities from the face of Him, the Lord that sitteth upon the throne; yes, sitteth at the right hand of the Father!"

"Look, curate; don't become cross with me, just because I have meticulously cross-examined you," I seriously divulged, "because I believe that you might be an avowed cross-dresser who has coyly double-crossed your bishop, just like disloyal and traitorous Judas Iscariot had double-crossed your professed Lord and Messiah! And furthermore," I austerely emphasized, "I think that your fat-fuck, overfed bishop has all along double-crossed you with this litany of religious propaganda that you both espouse and maliciously perpetuate upon the gullible public! Chaucer be blessed! Your twisted cult language sounds a lot like some of the perverted Archbishop of Canterbury's tales."

I began to fully understand the cleric's ambivalent mental turmoil. My monologue temporarily ceased my labored endeavor at reasoning with the pathetic nitwit. I next struggled to my feet, and, standing over the dumb shit's bald head, I laid my hand upon his chubby shoulder, actually wanting to viciously beat the grieving, sanctimonious asshole to a pulp.

"Be a man!" I lectured to the woebegone zealot. "You're presently scared out of your fuckin' wits! What good is religion if it collapses under calamity? Think of what earthquakes and floods, not to mention countless wars and volcanoes, have done to mankind in the past! Did you think God had exempted Weybridge? He is not an insurance agent who casually tolerates humanity's plethora of billions and billions of accumulative mortal and venial sins!"

For a time, the dumbass fuckhead sat in blank silence. "But how can we escape?" the confused, quivering loon asked and sobbed. "Those brutal and soulless reptilians are invulnerable; the reprehensible monsters are pitiless."

"Were you bullied by kindergarten girls when you were in high school?" I rationally asked. "The mightier the Martians are, the more sane and wary of their false confidence we should be," I enunciated, sounding much like a fraudulent church minister myself. "A member of their kind had been killed, I believe, inside one of their downed walking forts over yonder; over in Shepperton, about three hours ago."

"Killed! Killed you say? My God, man! There is still hope for genuine salvation!"

"I saw it happen." Then, I proceeded to relate an additional detail. "All is not yet lost. St. Peter might still enroll your fat ass into his record book at the legendary Pearly Gates!"

"What is that constant flicker I've seen flashing up in the sky?" the weeping fellow curiously asked.

"Well, Reverend; it's definitely not perpetual light shining upon either you or me," I quite sarcastically pontificated. "What you've seen is the army's heliograph signaling, which are the signs of, a kind of semaphore, currently used in military communications. I believe that the latest message was that the Martian war machines are coming this way with intentions of attacking London."

And even as I spoke, the idealistic dumb-shit sprang to his feet and stopped me by a weird gesture. "Listen!" the suspected pedophile faggot uttered. "Do you hear what I hear, even though we're several thousand miles from the little town of Bethlehem!"

From beyond the low hills across the water came the dull resonance of distant guns, accompanied by the remote shouts and cries of apprehensive army fighting men. And after everything else became still, a symbolic black raven or crow came swooping-down over the high hedge and speedily flew past us. In the west, on the horizon, the rising crescent moon hung faint and pale above the dense smoke that was spiraling-up from twin towns Weybridge and Shepperton, the distasteful pollution completely neutralizing the hot, still, splendor of the sunset.

"We had better follow this path to our right," I suggested to the distressed and exasperated clergyman, with my bleeding index finger pointing northward.

Chapter 14

"LONDON"

My younger brother had been living in London when the Martians had virtually incinerated all of Woking. Harry "Har" Wells was a medical student diligently studying for an imminent senior-year examination at the London Mortuary Academy, and he had heard nothing of the alien arrival until late Saturday morning. The newspaper headlines contained, in addition to lengthy special articles describing the planet Mars, informative articles on the possibility of intelligent life flourishing on other planets inside our Solar System.

'I suppose that it's good that Harry's into embalming and not bombing,' I chuckled to myself. 'My younger brother is a conscientious objector and refuses to enter the army, even if it means the nation surrendering to the bastard alien aggressors.'

The Martians, being alarmed at several landing locations with the approach of curious crowds of 'death wish assholes', had killed a number of people with several quick-firing concussion guns, which apparently gave the onlookers terrible head concussions that caused instant, massive, cerebral strokes.

The London *Morning Telegram* concluded with the words: "Formidable as the dangerous rogues seem to be, the Martians on the Horsell Common have not moved from inside the pit into which their meteor machine had fallen, and, indeed, the enemy seems incapable of climbing-out. This is probably due to the relative strength of the earth's greater gravitational pull."

Of course, all the students in the Academy's embalming class, to which Harry had attended that day, were intensely interested in cramming for their major exam, but there were no signs of any unusual excitement or panic in the busy London streets. The afternoon papers teased scraps and bits of tantalizing news that typically appeared under sensational headlines. The main city tabloids had nothing of merit to report beyond the movement of troops maneuvering about the Horsell Common, and also, the "environmentally unsound" burning of the forest between Woking and Weybridge.

But then, the very reputable *St. James's Gazette*, in an extra-special evening edition, announced the bare fact of the interruption of telegraph communications between certain towns in the south. This was thought to be due to the falling of burning pine trees severing the pole lines. Nothing more of the interplanetary fighting was known that night, the eve of my dogcart drive to Leatherhead, and then back to Maybury Hill.

From later conversations, my brother felt no anxiety about my specific plight, since Harry knew from the newspaper columns that the first cylinder had descended a good mile and a half from my Maybury home. Har had made-up his mind to travel down by train that night to visit me, in order, as he *later* said, to see "the Things" before the army swiftly sent the moral-less invaders speeding into the cryptic Martian afterlife.

I also *later* learned that my favored brother had dispatched a telegram, which had never reached me, around about four o'clock, and Harry had spent the evening at the Albert Music Hall, listening with pleasure to classical Beethoven and Bach symphonies.

In London, also, on Saturday night, there was a heavy thunderstorm, and my "privileged brother" had reached Waterloo Station in a cab. On the platform from which the midnight express to Woking usually starts its route, Harry learned, after some waiting, that "a rail accident" had been preventing trains from reaching Woking. The exact nature of the "incident" my brother could not ascertain; indeed, the bureaucratic railway authorities did not even clearly know the particulars at that time.

There was very little excitement inside Waterloo Station, as the transportation officials, failing to realize that anything further than a minor breakdown between Byfleet and Woking junction had occurred, were *not* running the 'late theater trains', which usually passed southbound through Woking.

The railroad executives were busy making the necessary arrangements to alter the paths of the Southampton and Portsmouth Sunday Soccer League excursions, where in already-obliterated Woking, the first important soccer game of the regular season was supposed to kick-off against visiting Leatherhead.

A nocturnal newspaper reporter, mistaking my brother for the railroad traffic manager, tried interviewing Harry about the war in the south. Few people, except several low-level railway administrators, had correctly connected the suburban breakdown with the Martians' planet grab.

As for myself, in my concurrent journey to London, I had heard from itinerant travelers fleeing north, of separate hostile events in the Woking area, that on Sunday morning, "All London was electrified by the shocking news from Woking." As a matter of fact, to my personal experience, at the time, there was nothing to justify *that* very extravagant commentary.

Plenty of Londoners did not hear or care of the Martians until the frenetic panic of Monday morning. Those who did hear renditions from others took some time to realize and comprehend all of the hastily-worded dispatches conveyed in the morning papers. The majority of Londoners do not read the Sunday tabloids, but prefer to stay in bed and enjoy obtaining multiple orgasms, or prefer snoring and sleeping-off intoxication.

I remember thinking, 'Great coffins and embalming fluid! Har is probably more concerned about profiting from the hereafter without even giving a single thought as to what the fucked-up Martians are here after!'

About seven o'clock last night, the conniving Martians had furtively exited the Horsell Common cylinder, and, moving about under a protective armor of metallic shields, had completely wrecked the remainder of Woking Station, along with the adjacent whorehouses, and the interplanetary reptilian thugs also had massacred an elite battalion of the Cardigan Red Sweater Regiment.

No details were publicly known, or had been officially confirmed by the laconic military.

"Army cavalry riders have been galloping into downtown Chertsey," one vociferous asshole yelled to Harry at the Waterloo Station. "Make dust or be dust!"

The Martians appeared to be moving slowly towards the recently-installed railroad ties in downtown Chertsey, or possibly preparing for an offensive knot in Windsor. I read in the press that great anxiety had prevailed in West Surrey, in Curry, and in Marmalade, and high earth mounds were being built-up to check the advance of the "upcoming London onslaught".

That was how the often-erroneous *Sunday Sun* had documented the defensive measures taken to guard against the approaching Martian attack, and a clever-but-satirical depiction in the "handbook" section of the *London Referee Soccer Journal* compared the goals of the "writhing-but-*slug*-gish Martians" to a "zoo menagerie suddenly let loose inside a placid, rural village such as Chertsey".

The money-hungry Sunday papers printed separate late editions as further news came to the editors' attention. But there was practically nothing more to inform the mostly-apathetic and lethargic city population until late in the afternoon, when the authorities gave the mass media agencies the limited, updated information in their possession.

It had been haphazardly stated in several of the brain-dead tabloids that the people of Walton and Weybridge, all regarded as part of the local "Walton Family", were pouring along the major roads leading toward London.

I *later* learned from Harry that on Sunday morning, my religious brother had attended church at the Foundling Hospital, but Harry had still been in ignorance of what had been happening in the south.

At the religious service, Harry had heard allusions made to the "fucked-up invasion", and a special prayer for peace and "killing the Martian dickheads" was led by the congregation's chief pedophile priest. Coming out from the church, "Digger", my brother's nickname, honored a hankering and bought a copy of *Referee*. My sibling became rather alarmed at the sensationalized front-page news, and quickly hastened again to Waterloo Station to find-out if telegraph communication with the city's suburbs had been restored.

The omnibuses, carriages, bicyclists, hansoms, and innumerable pedestrians who were casually strolling-about downtown in their finest Sunday clothes, seemed scarcely affected by the strange "science-fiction cartoon information" that the profit-oriented news vendors were disseminating.

On the congested Waterloo Station train platform, Harry heard that the Windsor and Chertsey express lines had been "temporarily interrupted". The porters had told Har that several remarkable telegrams had been received in the morning from the Byfleet and Chertsey stations, but those news dispatches had abruptly ceased being transmitted. Other than a few sketchy and vague reports, Harry could garner very little precise details, and later, my frustrated brother had told a rookie journalist for the avant-garde *Rolling Stone Late Gazette,* "I can't get no fuckin' satisfaction!".

The train service was then very much disorganized, especially unable to satisfy the adamant complaints of inconvenienced daily passengers having one-track minds. Quite a number of people who had been expecting friends or relatives from places on the South-Western networks were standing about Waterloo, wishing that utilitarian flush toilets had been invented.

According to Harry's *later* testimony, one grey-headed, elderly curmudgeon in his presence came-over and bitterly abused the on-duty South-Western Company representative. "This lousy railroad is railroading us. The investors are mostly green energy assholes who don't like the idea of the locomotives burning coal and polluting the atmosphere!" the fossil-faced geezer insisted. "As Shakespeare once said, you' assholes have got to get your Act together!"

"But green energy hasn't been invented yet!" eavesdropping Harry challenged the old fart.

"Yeah, but I'll bet that those little green men from Mars have already cut a deal with the railroads to sell that green energy bullshit to the train union's members and also, to the capitalistic company brass for a handsome profit!"

One or two passenger trains had arrived at Waterloo from Richmond, Putney, and Kingston, and the excursions had transported irate, garrulous passengers who had gone-out for a day's boating, and found the canal locks closed with no official government explanation being provided. A man in a blue and white blazer addressed my brother, and his narrative was full of strange suburban revelations.

"There are hosts of people driving into Kingston in buggies and carts, with boxes of their valuables being carried to safety," the veteran carnival barker announced. "They're coming from Molesey, Weybridge and Walton, and the train riders say there's been heavy cannon fire heard at Chertsey, and that mounted soldiers have earlier told the passengers to 'get the hell out of harm's way at once because the Martians are coming, and I don't mean that they're having perverted sex with one another'!"

"Maybe the British artillery units are *cannonizing* captured Martians and making them into heavenly saints!" Harry joked. "And if the smart-ass aliens ever make it to Wimbledon, the greedy eight-arm octopus shitheads can serve barbecued tennis balls to the hungry players standing in the popular breakfast line!"

After the old fogey departed to the stairs descending to street level, Harry realized that the talkative old fart was his girlfriend's voyeur-gynecologist, Dr. Claude Bush, who had recently retired because the feeble physician had been suffering from a severe case of tunnel-vision.

Around five in the afternoon, the church bells were ringing to signify the advent of evening prayer, and a squad of Salvation Army lassies came singing for charity donations down heavily-trafficked Waterloo Road. On the bridge, a number of idle loafers were watching a curious muddy scum layer drifting down the Thames, seemingly arranged and floating in stinky, brown patches. The sun was just setting, and the Westminster Clock Tower and the Houses of Parliament appeared very august, contrasted against one of the most peaceful, majestic skies one can ever imagine.

At that Parliament section of London, an army reservist quietly told my brother that he had seen the heliograph flickering-flashes in the west.

And then, on Wellington Street, Harry encountered a couple of sturdy roughnecks who had just rushed out of Fleet Street with newspaper headlines tucked under their arms. "Dreadful catastrophe!" the first ruffian was bawling. "Intense fighting going on at Weybridge!"

"Repulse the marauding Martians! London is in grave danger!" the second drunken barroom bully was bellowing. "Let's kick their asses good and pretend that their rear ends are soccer balls!"

It was then that Harry realized and acknowledged the full power and terror of those menacing invading monsters, who were being described on downtown message boards as "Vast spider-like machines, nearly a hundred-feet-high, capable of moving at the speed of an express train, and fully able to shoot-out a beam of intense heat that incinerates people into ashes."

According to various street conversations and general hearsay, a large number of army field guns had been stationed in the vicinity of Horsell Common, and especially positioned between the already-demolished Woking district and London.

According to London gossip, five of the alien machines had been reported moving towards the Thames, and another one had been destroyed near the Wey River. Most of the militia's artillery shells had missed their targets, and many of the veteran army batteries had been easily annihilated by the deadly green Heat-Ray. Heavy losses of soldiers were mentioned on the ever-changing, scribbles being pinned on the downtown message boards, but the tone of the general gossip was still optimistic, based on British stereotypes of *our* military's reputed excellence, and also on escalating patriotic fervor.

A reporter from the *Daily Gazette* gave Harry a confidential synopsis of the Martians relentless and tenacious military campaign. "The vile creatures had been repulsed at several suburban locations. The freakin' aliens are not invulnerable. The cowards had retreated to their triangle of cylinders, in the irregular circle about Horsell Common. Signalers with heliographs were pushing forward upon the hideous entrenched shits, and our troops are surrounding the enemy on all sides."

"What about the cannons and our highly-touted artillery defenses?" Harry asked the rather loquacious journalist. "What's the latest on that?"

"Gun positions have been deployed along the rapid transit line from Windsor, Portsmouth, Aldershot, and Woolwich. Altogether, there are reports of one hundred and sixteen blasters being in position, or being hastily placed, chiefly covering London and vicinity. Never before in England has there ever been such a vast mobilization of military material and personnel."

"Do you think that dynamite would effectively work against the lousy bastards?" Harry asked. "The ugly octopus-like son-of-a-bitches need to be thwarted and blasted from here to eternity."

"Any further cylinders that will fall, it is hoped that the competent commanding officers could destroy the space vehicles and their occupants by using high explosives, which were being rapidly distributed. Don't you think that that's a dynamite idea?"

"Sounds like Queen Victoria might be nominated for the Nobel Peace Prize," Harry cleverly jested. "That is, if Queen Victoria ever becomes victorious."

From further questioning the bullshitting newspaper scribe, the future undertaker learned that the Prime Minister had been informed by our best generals that from the size of the crashed cylinders, there could not be more than five occupants working in each unit, a grand total of perhaps fifteen Martians altogether.

"A million British troops versus no more than twenty-five fucked-up reptilians. Perhaps Parliament could send-out a few dozen navy frogmen to perform amphibian operations against the slithery fucks," Harry preposterously joked to the accommodating newspaper reporter.

All down Wellington Street, curious pedestrians could be seen reading every bit of news becoming available, and the Strand was suddenly noisy with the voices of army personnel shouting potential evacuation directions if everyone had to promptly abandon the city.

Going on along the Strand toward Trafalgar Square, my information-hungry brother encountered a few of the fugitives that had arrived from West Surrey. A family consisting of a husband, his wife, and two grammar school aged boys all had lugubrious expressions on their sooty faces. The grim visages of those harrowed refugees were exceedingly haggard, and their entire general appearance contrasted rather conspicuously with the Sabbath-best demeanor of the myriad devil-may-care Londoners who were casually riding inside the fancy avenue omnibuses.

"Where are you from? What's going on there? You look spent and fatigued?" my brother asked the distressed husband.

"We're from Surrey, and my wife and I are scared shitless. What we saw of the enemy would make Dracula stay permanently inside his macabre coffin!"

"Holy vamps in Transylvania!" the aspiring mortician exclaimed. "The Martians could scare the feces out of Dracula and Frankenstein, together. The invaders sound a thousand times more dangerous than commonplace vampires, zombies and fictional human monsters."

Beyond Buckingham Palace, the public-whorehouses and gay and lesbian sex parlors were still doing a lively trade. The popular sex-merchant venues were still attracting their normal clientele, since Harry was keenly aware from his personal experiences that biological gratification often trumps inevitable death and taxes.

At that volatile time, Har later reported that there had been a strong presence of shouting pedestrians scurrying about the streets, insisting that the government authorities were to blame for their incapacity to dispose of the satanic invaders, without causing all of the ostensible, unnecessary inconvenience.

At Piccadilly, Harry ran into an old friend just leaving a theatrical performance, and the fellow was actually a gay LBGT acquaintance, who had acquired the appropriate nickname "Big Benny", and coincidentally, operated the large clock atop Westminster Tower.

"What the hell's happening on the city's outskirts?" Harry asked his faggot friend. "Are any more Martian killing machines being brutally pulverized?"

'I don't know, and I don't fuckin' care," Big Benny replied. "I got a bottle of delectable scotch in my coat pocket, and I'm gonna' now visit the Cockney Homo Sapien Bar, find a muscular male companion, and then paint the whole goddamned town red! Tonight, Harry, I really don't give a shit about anything else."

Feeling restive, my obdurate brother walked all around that part of London, and finally, paced from Westminster Abbey over to his apartment near Regent's Park at about two in the morning. Harry's mind was in a neurotic state of flux, and in his lengthy hike, my brother had thought about the phenomenal "boilers on stilts" that were a fantastic hundred-feet-high, which was the general description being shared among strangers and friends in various street conversations.

'Tomorrow I'm scheduled to take my mortuary course exam,' my studious brother imagined. 'If we ever win this war of the worlds, then how the hell am I supposed to perform friggin' autopsies on the damned Martians? I wouldn't even know where the hell to find their dicks, testicles, tits, and slimy assholes!'

Harry's room was an attic garret, and he did not sleep soundly that night upon his hard mattress. At five a.m., my brother heard downtown church bells ringing and clanging inordinately. As my sibling thrust his head out the attic window, up and down the street, a dozen other heads were simultaneously sticking-out of neighbors' opened windows.

"They are coming!" boomed a petulant policeman's voice, as the sergeant was incessantly hammering at a door to wake-up the residents inside. "The damned Martians are coming!"

The sound of drumming and trumpeting came loudly from the Albany Street Barracks, and every church within earshot was hard at work disturbing everyone's sleep with dissonant bell knelling in its steeple. There was a distinct noise of doors opening and banging shut, and window after window in the adjacent houses flashed from darkness into yellow illumination.

"What the fuck is all that yelling down there?" an inebriated, old whiskerando boisterously hollered-down from his upstairs apartment. "I need my sleep, and I don't fuckin' enjoy being bothered when I'm trying to snooze-away a decent drunk!"

For a long time, my younger brother stared-out of the attic window in blank astonishment, watching the excited policeman wildly pounding his fist at door after door, and redundantly delivering and repeating the same almost-incomprehensible message.

The sleepy occupants craned their heads out of the rowhouse windows, straining to hear what the policeman had been shouting. People in pajamas were coming-out of the side streets, and others were standing in groups at the corners, talking incessantly.

"What the devil is it all about?" said my brother's fellow lodger. "Are the people protesting? Did the queen just outlaw sex?"

The neighbor across the hall rushed into Harry's room and yelled, "London is in imminent danger of destruction! The Kingston and Richmond defenses have caved! Telegraph communiques describe extensive massacres occurring throughout the Thames Valley!"

Londoners, who had gone to bed on Sunday night oblivious and unassuming, were presently rudely awakened in the small hours of Monday morning, rousing to a vivid sense of formidable danger.

Harry promptly put on his regular university clothes, hustled downstairs, and quickly stepped-out of the apartment building. As his feet touched the sidewalk, just as the sky between the houses' parapets grew pink with the early dawn, my alarmed brother turned his attention to the southern heavens.

"Black Smoke!" his ears heard people yelling. "Black Smoke!" the panic-stricken nutcases reiterated.

The contagion of such a unanimous fear was inevitable among such fickle commoners. As my brother hesitated at the base of the door-step, Harry noticed a news-vendor anxiously approaching, and Har instinctively purchased an early morning paper. The energized hawker was soon speedily running-away with the rest of the street's frightened pedestrians, and in the meantime, selling his papers for a shilling each, as the lad continued his mad dash, his enterprise truly was a grotesque mingling of profit and panic.

And from the newspaper, my brother read the catastrophic commentary of the Army Commander-in-Chief:

> "The Martians are able to discharge enormous clouds of a black and poisonous vapor by means of powerful rockets. The aliens have completely smothered and suffocated our batteries, demolished Richmond, Kingston, and Wimbledon, and currently are advancing rather slowly-but-methodically towards downtown London, destroying everything on the way. It is impossible to stop them with our inferior weaponry. There is no safe haven from the Black Smoke and deadly Heat-Ray. Every man, woman, and child for himself, or herself. May God save us all!"

That was all that the front-page article read, but the bone-chilling message was more-than-enough to give everyone diarrhea. The entire population of the great city of six-million souls was then stirring, slipping, and running in search of a safe haven; presently, the metropolis was being evacuated *en masse,* northward.

"Black Smoke!" the pathetic voices cried. "Fire! Heat-Ray. Death Beam! What the hell is this shit all about?"

The bells in the neighboring church towers made a startling, jangling tumult; a vendor's wagon at the local intersection carelessly smashed into a speeding carriage, instantly killing the pulling horse; and amid a variety of shrieks and curses, against the water tank anchored on a high roof up the street, Harry's eyes discerned sickly, yellowish-orange lights, indicating that houses in the distance were then burning from numerous fires.

My brother heard loud footsteps frantically running and fleeing in all directions, with scores of traumatized and paranoid residents fleeing and trampling-over others while shouting expletives like "Oh shit!" and "Fuck!"

Harry's wrinkle-faced landlady came to her front door, loosely wrapped in her dressing gown and shawl; the woman's equally-confounded husband followed her exit, both wondering what the hell kind of emergency had been occurring.

Thus, this narrative represents the vivid recollection of Harry "Har" Wells, exactly as my brother had articulated London activities that frightening weekend, when we had finally reunited at a later date.

Chapter 15

"EVENTS IN SURREY"

It was while the portly curate had sat and talked so irrationally to me under the high hedge in the flat meadows near Halliford, and concurrently, my brother Harry was watching the neurotic fugitives from the south stream across Westminster Bridge, that the maniacal Martians had resumed their offensive carnage.

As far as I could ascertain from the conflicting accounts being debated throughout the region below the Thames, the majority of the Martian machines remained busy with preparations around the Horsell pit until nine that night, surreptitiously hurrying like killer bees while enacting some secret evil operation, that ultimately, disengaged huge volumes of concentrated green smoke into the atmosphere, which really prolifically pissed-off the asinine local environmentalists.

But without delay, three fully-assembled alien units rose from the crescent around the Horsell pit, and advancing slowly and cautiously to the north, made their persistent way through Byfleet and Pyrford, and subsequently moving towards Ripley and Weybridge.

Soon, the colossal robots (perhaps occupied by skilled pilots) came in sight of the army batteries steadfastly waiting in position. The militant Martian monstrosities accelerated in a straight line, each unit being perhaps a mile and a half from its nearest companion. The awesome machines amazingly communicated with one another by means of transmitting siren-like howls, their uncanny "Atoo! Atoo! Atoo!" tones running-up and down the scale from one dissonant note to another.

It was this disturbing howling, along with the firing of the seemingly sterile army guns at Ripley, and at St. George's Hill, that had been heard at Upper Halliford. The Ripley gunners, unseasoned artillery rookies, prematurely fired their initial wild blast, and being inexperienced and fearing death, quickly bolted on horse and on foot through the already-deserted village. The mind-boggling mobile fort, using its incomparable Heat-Ray, walked serenely over the abandoned army guns, and a mile ahead, trespassed-upon and unexpectedly crushed the additional abandoned cannons in Painshill Park.

The St. George's Hill battery, however, contained seasoned veterans, who were better trained to adroitly defend their designated combat zone. Hidden inside the cover of the dark pine woods, the soldiers believed that their detection had been safe from enemy scrutiny. The on-a-mission squads confidently fired their guns and munitions at about a thousand yards range.

The shells flashed all-round the first elevated Martian contraption, and assuming that the targeted object had occupants manipulating its intricate functions, the apparatus staggered, and slowly dropped to one knee.

An exuberant soldier in the veteran St. George battery reported a positive comment to an assigned war correspondent, "The Martians are wimpy assholes! We can kick their butts before the feckless shits have a chance to ever use their green Heat-Ray, or their white Disintegration Beam!"

Everybody in the army artillery regiment that had been hidden among the trees enthusiastically cheered together, and their mighty guns were reloaded in frantic haste. The overthrown Martian machine sent-out a mysterious prolonged harsh, vibrant, distress signal, and almost immediately, the second glittering giant answered the odd auditory communication.

One of the tripod legs on the downed unit had been smashed by a lucky army shell. The next volley from St. George troops flew wide of the standing-but-tilted damaged hulk, and, simultaneously, both its remaining two-leg Heat-Ray guns blasted the condemned army batteries right into another dimension. The only survivor of the conflict had been the fortunate newspaper reporter, who had left the calamitous scene several minutes prior.

Astonishingly, the broken tripod leg had been fully repaired and again battle worthy in a matter of minutes. The three healthy enemy units seemed to be in a sort of rugby huddle, apparently reviewing combat strategy, and the army scouts who were watching the strange conference reported that the trio remained absolutely stationary for the next half-minute.

A technician of sorts tediously crawled-out of its enclosure; the creature was a small grey figure, probably a subordinate mechanic checking the recently installed spare parts of the now-fixed metallic knee-hinge. The alien technician had quickly finished his cursory inspection assignment, and the weird-looking shit reentered the leg's protective hood, which automatically closed in a very precision-like manner.

"Well, at least we now know that the lethal machines aren't the Martians," the commander in charge of the remaining battery related to his loyal lieutenant. "Now Corporal Fitting," Captain Wilson commanded, "be my courier and deliver an important message to Colonel Parkhurst. Tell him that the tripod machines are not the Martians. Instead, the enemy we've just observed looks something like a short grey monkey, at least the repairman, or robot, who we saw fixing the downed unit's knee replacement. There might be other Martians that have tentacles and octopus features as has been reported by civilian observers! Go quickly, Fitting, before the evil assholes shoot the Heat-Ray at this exposed position!"

It was a few minutes past nine that night when these same three alien sentinels were joined by three other mobile Martian powerhouses, each one carrying a lengthy, thick, black tube. Similar tubes were soon distributed to each of the original three immense moving forts, and the six war mechanisms proceeded in lockstep like parade soldiers, advancing along a curved line between St. George's Hill, Weybridge, and the village of Send, southwest of Ripley.

"What the hell are those black tubes?" Colonel Parkhurst asked Sergeant Ransom. "I'm sure the new-fangled things have some sinister intentions."

"If you want to know the truth, Colonel," Ransom bravely answered and nervously cleared his throat, "I think the whole black pipe exchange we had just witnessed symbolizes that shortly, you, me, and our entire company will soon be going down the tubes!"

A dozen rocket volleys sprang-out of the nearby hills, warning the waiting batteries around Ditton and Esher to be on red alert. At the same time, three of the original six fighting machines, now armed with the enigmatic black tubes, waded across the nearby tributary, and two of the behemoths, shadowy against the western sky, came into sight of myself and the curate as we wearily hurried our asses off, sprinting along the road that runs northward out of Halliford.

The enemy contrivances moved onward, disregarding us as if we were "small potatoes", but otherwise, behaving much like a team of stalking hunting hounds searching-out a family of foxes.

At seeing that amazing sight, the nervous curate's throat cried faintly, and the intimidated asshole began pissing and crapping his black trousers. But I knew it was no good to run from a Martian Death-Ray, so I turned aside, knelt-down, and crawled through dewy nettles and brambles into the nearby ditch. The craven clergyman looked back, and with empty kidneys and an empty colon, noticed what I was doing. The dumb-shit turned and scampered back to join me.

"Now I know what it means when people say they're frightened to death! I'm scared shitless!" the psycho church assistant whimpered.

"You're right about having an empty anus!" I attested. "Now you no longer will be able to have your bowels in an uproar! But at least you've gotten most of the stenchy waste out of your pathetic body!"

"I don't want to die or be bludgeoned!" the curate sobbed. "My vital service to the Lord would then be too abbreviated!"

"Look here, Reverend! Christ had sacrificed His life on Calvary to purge your litany of sins from your soul," I rankled. "And you probably complain when you only sacrifice for Lent eating guacamole, or something trivial like that, because in truth, you're nothing but a pusillanimous fool, who more-than-likely is allergic to guacamole, and more-than-likely, never eats avocados, anyway! Get a fuckin' life, will ya'!"

"Please have mercy," the curate begged. "I'm frightened beyond belief, and I truly don't want to die!"

"Don't worry," I sarcastically replied. "My brother's a mortician, and he'll take adequate care of your obese corpse, so that you can rise from your shallow grave and be resurrected on Judgment Day as the Bible has prescribed. Are you questioning your Christian faith?"

The curate cupped his grimy hands to his face and had not the will to say any words or phrases.

"Just remember!" I sternly stressed and lectured. "These fucked-up Martians know or care nothing about your Holy Bible; about Moses; about God the Father Almighty; about Henry the Eighth and the Anglican Church, or about, Abraham, Jacob, and Isaac, or about your revered Savior and Messiah! The aliens don't even give a shit whether or not Mary Magdalene was a virgin, or whether the presumed prostitute had ever been secretly married to Jesus Christ!"

"Bless you, my son! You are wiser than Socrates!"

"Look, Reverend. Don't swallow-down any of the wet mud inside this ditch, or you might wind-up with a bad case of trench-mouth! But keep your body intact so that you can have a Christian burial and be raptured into the clouds on Judgment Day. If you are maliciously disintegrated by the Martians' deadly Heat-Ray, your ashes will be scattered all over, and you might not have an intact body to be raptured into Heaven!"

Never since the devising of gunpowder was the beginning of a battle so still and suspenseful. The cleric and I both felt like singing "Silent Night", even though Christmas had been celebrated several months before.

These authentic descriptions being revealed had been gleaned from various conversations that I had had with wandering survivors hiding in the shrubbery; from rural towns I had visited on my strenuous trek toward London, and from information I had obtained from stuttering military couriers with whom I had conferred, or from newspaper reporters who were cooperative in sharing their secret information.

"I'm afraid to die!" the penitent curate confessed and cried," as if I were an ordained priest hearing his last confession. "If I'm disintegrated by the green Heat-Ray, my soul won't ever qualify for admission to either Purgatory or Limbo!"

"What the hell do you want me to do?" I angrily declared. "I'm not a fuckin' minister, so don't expect any damned absolution from me! Put your big boy white collar on, and this time, don't crap or piss into your pants! If you want to gain Paradise and appear before the Lord, you can't stink to High Heaven!"

No doubt, in retrospect, the thought that had been uppermost in those puzzling alien intelligences was the supreme riddle of how much the heartless fucks understood about our strengths and our weaknesses. Did the invaders grasp that millions of military and civilian mortals were somewhat organized, disciplined, and working together to defeat their asses? Or did the robotic shits accurately interpret our spurts of retaliatory fire; or comprehend the pertinent stinging of our mortar shells; or fathom our steady surveillance of their encampment, or imagine that our forces were planning counter-attack "sting operations", and that the human race was set to act as a furious hive of on-a-mission, belligerent bees?

"Do the immoral invaders actually dream of exterminating every one of us?" the almost-delirious curate whimpered as we again crouched-down on our knees in the very wet and soggy ditch. "Will the brutes take prisoners and use those unfortunate captives as slaves?"

"Obviously, I believe that the nasty shits will need to establish vital supply chains for additional munitions and energy sources necessary to generate their deadly green rays and white beams," I logically replied to the petrified clergyman. "Also, the invaders need to address the basic necessities of food and fresh water. If you ever encounter a Martian face-to-face," I advised the distraught curate, "make sure that the last thing you would say out of utter contempt and anger would be 'eat me'!"

"I'll remember that axiom!" the despondent church assistant grieved. "If I courteously offered the vile son-of-a-bitches

Communion, I speculate that the nearest savage would be liable to bite my hand and dick off!"

"Well, Padre. I'm glad that you're discarding your pompous, sanctimonious, holier-than-thou demeanor, along with your lofty vernacular, and presently. you're starting to sound a bit like me. All you have to now conquer is your annoying, self-sympathy sniveling."

Our verbal exchange was rudely interrupted with the sounds of distant artillery bursts. Much to our ascending dread, a Martian machine stealthily approached through the nearby woods and raised *its* black tube, which soon emitted a powerful discharge that made the ground tremble and heave-up.

The landscape around Staines, a mile to the north, instantaneously inundated and collapsed, with the entire town quickly vanishing into a newly-formed, deep, subterranean cavern. Amazingly, there was no flash, no warning green smoke, but simply a distant, very potent detonation that caused the entire community to be gulped-down into the earth, all at once.

My mind was so much in turmoil after witnessing the tremendous catastrophe that I ignored both my personal safety and also my scalded hands, and I clambered-up into the hedge above the hidden ditch to survey the topography over towards Sunbury.

As I irresponsibly did so, a second silent invisible beam was shot from the ominous black tube, and instead of being vaporized, Sunbury experienced a similar fate that had happened to formerly somnolent Staines, sinking deep into the ground.

"What the fuck happened?" asked the bewildered curate, standing-up in the mud, and now sounding like a normal British working-class citizen instead of a pretentious, egocentric, narcissistic pig.

"Heaven knows; if there is indeed a caring Heaven, it must be on vacation!" I philosophically answered. "I believe we've just witnessed a third state-of-the-art weapon being deployed, besides the devastating Heat-Ray and the deadly White Beam, which now both seem to be almost obsolete items in the aliens' awesome arsenal. In a religious, ritualistic sense, it's like inventing Communion to override the sacraments of Baptism and Confirmation!"

"I think you're being excessively sacrilegious!" my reformed companion reverted to his old self. "You're talking like an apostate!"

"You have no balls!" I angrily reprimanded the curate. "You were probably one of those Castrati choir boys I had read about in a fucked-up Oxford University undergraduate history course that I had been required to take! Balls said, the queen; if I had them, I'd be king!"

"Look asshole," fired-back the changed-in-personality and altered-character cleric. "Tell that same fuckin' erroneous bullshit to Queen Victoria! And Her Majesty would promptly order her royal guards to make *you* into a fucked-up Castrati choir boy, even growing tits!"

"Sounds like you have too much Aristophanes on your Plato!" I sarcastically joked.

"Well then," the irascible curate started to ask. "What the hell would you call an adult who has had his balls sliced-off?"

"Eunuch!" I carefully pronounced.

"No, my goddamned name is Bartholomew, but by coincidence, my middle name happens to be Nicholas!" the ambivalent cleric nastily admonished and clarified.

Our erudite, oratorical discourse was then distracted by a bat flapping its wings and flickering above our inane conversation, and then vanishing in the opposite direction from already-doomed Sunbury. I heard in the far distance a tumult of shouting soldiers, which almost simultaneously ceased when another area of landscape was suddenly swallowed-up into the Earth.

I looked again at the tall Martian machine standing several-hundred-feet away, with its back to where I had been keenly peering, and my astounded eyes observed that the juggernaut was beginning to move eastward along the Thames towards London.

The figure of the on-the-move Martian grew smaller as the colossus receded further into the valley, until the contraption was no longer distinguishable. By a common impulse, Bartholomew, for that was the curate's formal first name, and I clambered to a higher elevation. Then, across the river, near Walton, we observed another such sunken terrain where proud Sunbury had once been.

Everything in the air had suddenly become very still. Far away to the southeast, marking the eerie quietness, "Bart" and I together heard the Martians hooting their strange language in indecipherable syllables to one another, and then the air quivered again with the distant thud of impotent army guns, which ten seconds later were silenced as a result of the implementation of the Martians' fatal black tube.

Bart pointed-out to me a plausible observation that had eluded my thinking. The horrific black tubes, after efficiently sinking a town or village into a deep pit, the mammoth destructive weapons also would next cause a toxic vapor to arise out of the massive hollow and poison the lungs of any human who had survived the submerging calamity, on the plunging town's outer perimeter.

"I thought that lengthy, loud, fat ladies' farts breathed in on the London-bound trains produced a terrible malodor," Bartholomew weirdly articulated, "but this new odorless gas that the Martians are using must be ten times as sickening as that hydrogen-sulfide stench that my prank-happy instructor would deliberately produce in my chemistry lab over at Eton. Just look at all the motionless corpses lying outside Sunbury!"

"Right Bart," I concurred. "The only good aspect to those science class pungent 'rotten egg' demonstrations was that the students could silently fart all the hell they wanted, and nobody else in the classroom would know the damned difference."

Then, a familiar streak in the night sky indicated that another interplanetary cylinder, a brilliant green meteor, was about to have a crash-landing in Bushey Park, where up to just last week, kinky strippers would often show their hairy beavers to wealthy, horny males, who were willing to pay ten pounds apiece.

As the army guns situated on the Richmond and Kingston hills began blasting their worthless shells, the deadly green vapor easily overwhelmed the gunners, without the wretched Martians ever activating their town-sinking, indispensable black tubes.

The ruthless Martians spread their stifling toxic vapors over all the hills and dales leading towards London, and Hanwell, Coombe, and Malden, all lying in the enemy's path, were doomed to be systematically eradicated. Even the new heavy artillery at St. George's Hill had been *brought-down* like duckpins at a bowling green, with all of the operational troops being cruelly gassed to death.

"Our forces would stand more of a chance of winning the Irish Sweepstakes than to defeat these irrepressible, other world bastards in combat," I opined to my traveling colleague. "Our only chance against the implacable Martians, Bart, is to introduce the son-of-a-bitches to lottery betting, raffles, scotch whiskey, porno' mags, venereal diseases, and tawdry circus freak shows."

"Well, Herbert George," Bartholomew enunciated, and then even shocked *my* corrupt vulgar sensitivities. "I believe and agree that mortal and venial sins like lust, pride, envy, sloth and greed, in addition to various venereal diseases like gonorrhea, herpes and syphilis, will eventually kill the dirty mother-fuckers in the long run!"

Sunday night was the end of the battered army's organized opposition to the unstoppable Martian military aggression. Even the heralded coastal torpedo-boat crews and navy war destroyers, waiting at the mouth of the Thames, were, according to scuttlebutt, being decisively trounced.

One has to imagine, as well as one may, the fate of those remaining batteries positioned towards Esher, waiting so tensely in the twilight, only to be annihilated by poisonous gas, like a nest of targeted cockroaches being casually sprayed. Survivors, there were none, to which to tally or account.

Hospital tents were overcrowded, and the besieged medical staffs were overwhelmed, attempting to treat the myriad burned and wounded victims, just alone, coming from the diabolical Weybridge debacle. Then later, the dull resonance of additional Martian blasts had been discerned, originating in center city London, and the outmatched army's clumsy projectiles were whirling overhead, haphazardly aimed towards Martian machines that were completely invulnerable to obliteration.

Before dawn, the dreadful odorless vapor had been pouring through the streets of Richmond, and the cowardly, fat, bald-headed Parliament politicians, with a last expiring effort, instructed the city's police precincts to begin rousing the population of London to engage in rapid flight, channeling the frenetic masses to either Coventry or Manchester.

"What should we do, Herbert," Bartholomew asked in a hysterical tone. "How's the best way to escape these fucked-up maniacs?"

"Let's rob a handgun and some bullets from a fallen soldier's holster," I suggested. "And then Bart, we can play a short game of Russian roulette, and the first one who dies from receiving a lucky hole in the head will be declared the winner! As Eve said to Adam, 'How do ya' like them apples'!"

Chapter 16

"EXODUS FROM LONDON"

For a brief interval, the army gunfire along with the sophisticated Martian land maneuvers had ceased. I had been evaluating Bartholomew's gutless demeanor, and decided to confront the craven curate with my administration of a viable truth analysis.

"Bart, I think you're a feckless, contemporary Transcendentalist as opposed to myself, who believes that I'm an advocate of Reverse-Transcendentalism."

"What the hell are you talking about?" Bartholomew wondered and reflexively challenged. "I've never in my entire elite education heard of such unmitigated, academic bullshit. Who the hell invented such disingenuous horse manure? That American hypocrite, P.T. Barnum? How about Benedict Arnold?"

"Well, my dear Curate. Transcendentalism in America started around eighty or so years ago by two prominent New England philosophers, Henry David Thoreau and Ralph Waldo Emerson."

"I've heard of Thoreau, and appreciatively, I've read of his thorough experience at *Walden Pond,* which I had thoroughly enjoyed comprehending at Eton. The book, if I recall," Bartholomew garrulously equivocated, "was about self-sufficient, independently living alone in the woods, apart from society, and *Walden Pond* gave me much to ponder. But who the hell was Ralph Waldo Emerson?"

"Well, Bart; Ralph Waldo Emerson was the true founder of Transcendentalism, which has as its fundamental premise the notion that emotion should *transcend* reason. Now, I definitely think that you're a fucked-up Transcendentalism, because you behave in a maudlin and cowardly manner when directly confronted with struggle, failure, or possible defeat."

"So then, what the hell is Reverse-Transcendentalism? Is it a popular movement in the States? Isn't the world upside-down and totally fucked-up already, without being reversed or inverted?"

"Well, if you flip emotion and reason, then obviously, reason triumphs over feelings," I expounded. "You're *the* exception to being an individual thinker, because you fuckin' *feel* every abstract idea, rather than using your brain to logically deal with problems and issues that confront you. You're basically fucked-up, because you think emotionally, and not rationally. You believe religiously, and certainly not scientifically, not having full control and dominion over your vacillating emotions," I articulated. "That's why I'm a Reverse-Transcendentalist and you're a wimpy Transcendentalist who believes in mass 'group feeling', as contrary to acting as an independent-thinking individual. That's why Sunday church services are often referred to as a 'Mass', since you'd rather be a herded lamb than a shepherd, like the Archbishop of Canterbury and the Catholic Pope happen to be!"

The war fighting resumed, and its continuation interrupted our impromptu "trench symposium", and poor, befuddled Bart sat in the ditch's mud, staring blankly into the heavens as if in a major trance, with his tortured brain contemplating the deep metaphysical ideas we had just discussed.

With the distant booms, my addled brain visualized the roaring wave of fear that was sweeping through the greatest city in the world, starting at Monday morning's dawn. Viewing the areas streaming bright detonations to the north, I imagined that there was a great tumult occurring around Paddington and Waterloo, the principal London railway stations, which apparently had been bleeding-over into horrible in-progress conflagrations at the key shipping piers along the Thames. I also speculated that the police and the railroad organizations were losing coherency and control, and I plausibly theorized that the swift deterioration of stable London society was indeed disintegrating into turmoil.

The railway passengers north of the Thames, and the South-Eastern pedestrians around booming Cannon Street, all had been warned by midnight on Sunday to seek shelter to the north, and re-scheduled trains were hastily being filled by panicky "me first" and "get the hell out of my way" people.

I conjectured that many formerly benign residents were now fighting and punching savagely for "standing-room only" inside the loaded-to-capacity carriages. Other frantic Londoners were more-than-likely being trampled and crushed between Bishopsgate Street and the normally chaotic Liverpool Street Station; and police revolvers were more-than-likely being fired to regain order. I imagined innocent people being stabbed, and the disgruntled bobbies who had been sent-out to direct traffic and maintain law and order, were probably both exhausted and infuriated. The cops were no doubt on riot patrol, employing their night-sticks, and cracking-open the heads of violators whom the overwhelmed officers were originally called-out to protect.

According to the paranoid evacuees I had interviewed, by midday, a Martian machine had been seen at Barnes, and a cloud of slowly sinking black vapor had filtered-out along the Thames, and soon drifted across the flats of Lambeth, probably cutting-off all means of escape over the congested bridges.

After a fruitless-but-noble struggle to get aboard a North-Western train, Harry later told me that he had emerged upon the Chalk Farm Road, and then *Har* furiously dodged across the frenetic thoroughfare through a hurrying swarm of veering and weaving vehicles, and by good fortune, had ventured inside a chaotic bicycle shop.

The front tire of the bike that Harry had battled to confiscate had been punctured, and fighting-off three hysterical rivals, my brother initiated his faulty escape, fully realizing that his repugnant human rivals were almost as dangerous as the more-than-vitriolic Martians.

Har dragged the pilfered bicycle through the store's shattered front window, sustaining only a cut wrist in enacting his theft. My under-duress brother next peddled the partially-disabled bike into Belsize Road.

And so, the lucky fellow managed to avoid the ongoing fury and the wild sidewalk panic, and skirting the Edgware Road, Har reached the town center, with his mind and body in dual weary and desperate states. But Harry's advantage was negated by the bicycle's bent rim and flat tire, so my determined brother rather inelegantly jockeyed his way slightly ahead of the crazed, fleeing crowd.

Harry was passed by a number of cyclists pedaling fully-functional bikes, and also by five horsemen in flapping saddles ridding upon galloping steeds, and soon after, by two bouncing modern motor cars.

A mile from Edgware, the rim of the bike's front wheel broke and bent, and Har's escape machine instantly became useless. The disappointed rider left the disabled mode-of-transportation by the roadside, and trudged through the mostly-vacated small village square.

Accurate news of the London fiasco had yet to reach the remaining residents of the lazy suburban community, and half of Edgware's main street shops were still open for business, but empty of customers.

Curious residents soon left their apartments and rowhouses, and crowded onto the pavement, as if a major holiday parade were in progress, and the local folks were astonishingly staring at an extraordinary procession of migrating fugitives who had started flooding the main avenue.

For a time, Harry remained in Edgware, not knowing what to do next. The incensed evacuees, with thin-skinned temperaments, increased in number. Many of the escapees, like my brother, seemed inclined to loiter in the seemingly safe suburb to learn more about the Martians most recent maneuvers. At the time, there was no fresh news concerning the pernicious invaders to instill heightened street chaos and potential violence.

My brother had a vague idea of successfully making his way to Chelmsford, where some university friends lived, and that inclination at last induced my sibling to strike into a quiet lane running eastward. The perplexed fellow followed a narrow footpath leading northeastward. Much to his relief, Har encountered few fugitives until, in a grassy lane nearing High Barnet, my fatigued brother happened upon two upper-class ladies, who ironically, soon became his fellow travelers.

Harry had heard and was responding to their loud screams, and hustling around a bend, noticed two "me first" punks struggling to drag the helpless ladies out of their little pony-chaise in which the pair had been riding. One of the females, a short, slender woman dressed in white, was simply screaming for assistance; the other woman, an older dark-skinned figure, slashed at the more hostile mugger, who gripped her arm with the whip she was holding in her right hand.

My concerned brother immediately grasped the gravity of the situation, shouted, and hurried towards the scene of assault. One of the thugs turned towards the gallant rescuer, and realizing from the antagonist's face that a fight was unavoidable, and being an expert boxer, Harry violently and repeatedly smashed the assailant's skull against the chaise's frame.

It was no time for pugilistic chivalry, and my muscular brother easily laid the predacious asshole quiet with a karate kick to the jaw, and swinging his body around, gripped the collar of the other antagonist, who had vigorously been pulling the seated lady's arm.

During the fierce altercation, the older woman's whip stung across Harry's face when her arm had reached back in self-defense, and the cutthroat who Har had kicked to the road, groggily rose to his feet, and gaining his sense of balance, scampered alongside his equally injured accomplice down the lane in the direction from which the repulsive rogues had come.

"Take this!" said the pretty slender lady, as she handed my brother her revolver. "This pistol could deter other lowlife knaves from enacting their malice."

"Get back onto the chaise," my brother imperatively ordered, wiping the blood dripping from his split lip. "Your companion seems to be quite alarmed, and you should comfort her, whether you're both out-of-the-closet gay lovers or not!"

"Are you a boxer?" the impressed, thin lady asked.

"No, madam. I'm a human being and not a damned trained dog!"

"Then, you must be a professional wrestler the way you manhandled those vile villains?"

"Well, in my freshman year at college, I once had Admiral Nelson's great-grandson locked in a half-Nelson, and was able to pin the squirming son-of-a-bitch to the mat!" the avid punster disingenuously joked and fibbed. "My nickname was Punches Pilate!"

"I'll gladly give you the reins and the whip," the older lady stated, obviously enamored with my younger brother's physique. "You look quite strong and burly, and we need manly protection like yourself to keep us safe from nutcase highway thieves and irate scumbags."

So, quite unexpectedly, my brother found himself, panting, with a cut and swollen mouth, a bruised jaw, and bloodstained knuckles, driving along an unknown lane with 2 anonymous-but-appreciative, quite sophisticated, high-society ladies.

Har soon learned that the ladies were the wife and daughter of a well-to-do surgeon living in Stanmore, and the pair of females had been coming from having a recent visit to Pinner. And Harry heard from the two females a number of incredible rumors describing an interplanetary invasion at the Pinner Railway Station on their way back home.

Upon their arriving home at Stanmore, the doctor, a science-fiction enthusiast, immediately packed food and some other essential provisions, and hopefully, lovingly dispatched his wife and daughter off to board a train heading north to escape the advancing Martians.

The threesome, then seated in the petite chaise, stopped and made an improvised encampment by the wayside, and the pony became happy taking a lengthy leak in the natural high grass. Harry told the ladies of his own rapid escape out of London, and revealed all that he knew of the fucked-up Martians' nefarious ways.

"We have money," revealed the petite, slender daughter, and then hesitated, fearing that their escort might have a change in character and decide to pursue robbery. The pretty daughter's scared-but-trusting blue eyes met my handsome brother's curious stare. "We're carrying thirty pounds of gold and a five-pound note."

"So, I have about the same amount in my pants pocket," the new chaise driver divulged. "But I fear that soon, ladies, even money will be of no value or use, and seventy pounds will not be able to bribe others to render assistance, food, or shelter."

"That's more than enough we have together to board a train at St. Albans, or at New Barnet," the older, aristocratic woman suggested. "My skeptical mind thought that I had been witnessing a hopeless fantasy being dramatized, with my incredulous eyes seeing the fury of the fretful Londoners crowding upon the trains like an African wildebeest stampede. My sweet daughter posed her own plan of striking across Essex, thus, escaping the encroaching mayhem by leaving the country altogether, and eventually taking a steam ferry over to Europe."

"The Martians are relentless," my brother answered. "All that the barbaric fiends know is killing, conquest, and more killing!"

The older lady, Mrs. Elphinstone, formally introduced herself to Har, along with Dorothy, the younger female chaise passenger, being her comely daughter.

"Well, ladies," my likeable brother replied. "My theory is that these abominable Martians will soon be spontaneously landing on every single continent and known country all over the world. But right this minute, I just think that the treacherous aliens are only operating here in England. In my humble opinion, we would be safer traveling on Mars than right here on Earth."

"Several people in our village have said that the Martians look like vertical, walking alligators," Mrs. Elphinstone commented. "Please tell us Harry; have you heard similar reports?"

"The invaders don't look like vertical walking alligators. That's a croc. I've heard that a more likely description circulating around London is that the creatures look like grey octopuses having eight very ugly pusses, and that they've trained miniature, greyish-brown, robotic monkeys to act as their servants and technicians."

As the small carriage being pulled by the diminutive pony reached the Great North Road, the three garrulous riders began encountering more confused wanderers, seemingly moping-around in a group daze. For the most part, those befuddled dunderheads were staring upon the road with their faces against their chests, murmuring indistinct gibberish, and the human automatons appeared to be haggard, jaded, unkempt-looking zombies.

One brawny tattooed imbecile, apparently an esteemed LBGTQRSTUVW member, who was formally garbed in a silk evening gown and red high heels, clumsily passed the petite carriage, running on foot. "I'm desperately searching for my transgender mate!" the idiot boomed. "If you see her, she's wearing a white tuxedo, a tall top hat, and brandishing a black cane!"

"Good heavens!" cried Mrs. Elphinstone. "The houses up ahead are all on fire with no firehouses in sight, or any available firemen to extinguish the raging infernos. What is this insanity you are driving us into? It's worse than that Were-wolfs of London play that Dorothy and I attended at Piccadilly last week!"

Seeing possible danger approaching, my alert brother abruptly stopped the Lilliputian carriage. Then Har, who possessed a wonderful imagination, shouted to the pair of encroaching men, who greedily wanted to commandeer the small carriage, probably desiring to throw the three chaise occupants onto the road, and presumably, maliciously steal the pony-pulled vehicle for their own selfish use.

"Way!" my brother hollered. "Make way! These two women are both pregnant with triples, and I must immediately seek medical help. Make way, I say, or you might be splattered with grotesque amounts of disgusting afterbirth all over your ugly faces!"

The carriage sped by two surly, gay men, who looked like bodybuilding weightlifters, affectionately holding hands while waving small British LBGTQRSTUVW flags. Then, a dirty-faced woman, carrying a heavy bundle and loudly weeping, was nearly flattened by the careening chaise and almost instantly given "that run-down feeling".

So much as the three carriage occupants could see, the dingy cobblestone road contained a tumultuous stream of grimy, harried scumbags, potentially bent on erupting into total anarchy; the mass of bobbing black heads, looking like a sea of giant dark pimples, along with the crowded "me first" filthy anatomies obnoxiously pushing and shoving one another, all presented the rambunctious scene as escalating into a growing, imminent threat to the three vulnerable chaise riders.

"Go on! Go on!" cried the various voices. "Way! Way! Let those three dipshit assholes pass, all the way to the Wey!"

"Bedlam Hospital is like paradise compared to these crazed maniacs shouting and fighting all around us," Dorothy screamed as the bouncing carriage wove in and out of the surrounding human chaos. "I've never been so terrified in all my life! This is much more visceral than when I had my first monthly period last week!"

"You haven't seen anything yet if those vile, riotous cretins shrieking outside this carriage manage to pull you off and crush you under their mad rush to pilfer this chaise," Har shouted and informed. "I'm a mortician, but honestly, this escape is the biggest undertaking I've ever attempted!"

"You're an Undertaker?" Mrs. Elphinstone shrieked and gasped above the general havoc. "Christ! I'm more afraid of you than I am of these nutcase rioters, or of the atrocious alligator-skin Martians! I mean Harry; I'm an educated woman of high-society and fine culture, but I just gotta' ask your ass, what the fuck is happening to these crazy bastards and bitches, all delirious like wild baboons, and what about the incensed dumb-shit mob that's insanely endeavoring to attack us?"

"The shitheads think they're scrambling-around inside hell already," my brother yelled above the enveloping noise. "They're liable to scare the fuckin' Martians back home with their male and female hormone rantings, and the climax of their wild activity will sound like the biggest sex-orgy group orgasm in all of history!"

There were out-of-control cabs, carriages, shop-carts, wagons, an abandoned mail cart, and a road-cleaner's buggy that was marked "Vestry of St. Pancreas", all disabled and scattered about the road.

Soon, a huge timber-wagon loaded with roughnecks and clamorous hookers, and each whore was seeking one final trick before being sent directly to Satan's volcanic subterranean bordello. And finally, a brewer's dray rumbled-by with two male passengers chasing the runaway prostitutes in hot pursuit, wanting to get laid one final time before being vaporized straight into incomprehensible oblivion.

"Clear the way!" cried the two desperate jerk-offs. "Clear the way!"

Other lackluster, suddenly-religious assholes were chanting as the zany fools scurried-about, "Eter-nity! Eter-nity!" was the mantra that came echoing-down the road, which inspired Dorothy and Mrs. Elphinstone to inharmoniously bellow-out, "Mater-nity! Maternity! We're both giving birth from the same fuckin' father!"

A little old man, with a grey military moustache and a filthy black frock coat, limped-out from the side woods, and sat-down, removed his boot, and his sock, which was blood-stained. The elderly codger shook out a pebble, and hobbled-on again; and then a little girl of eight or nine, all alone, threw herself under the hedge close by a rhododendron bush, weeping incessantly.

"I can't go on! I can't go on!" cried Mrs. Elphinstone. "This misadventure is far worse than having sex for ten hours inside a small cage with an overgrown, nine-hundred-pound gorilla in heat."

"It's like a human zoo gone amok," Dorothy added. "Where are the fuckin' police? This shit-show menagerie needs lion-tamers, just like vast deserts need water!"

Ironically, a bizarre ignoramus ran parallel to the weaving carriage and yelled, "Where is there water?"

"Lord Garrick!" exclaimed my brother to petrified Dorothy and Mrs. Elphinstone. "That's Lord Garrick, the Chief Justice wearing his white wig!"

"Two antagonistic imbeciles began pounding the Chief Justice upon his white wig and also upon his ruddy face. "We don't give a mouse-turd who the hell you think you are!" the larger and taller unsavory ruffian yelled to eminent Lord Garrick. "Get the fuck out of our way before we knuckle you good!"

"Go on!" yelled the aroused and raucous rebels, also thrusting clenched fists at the Chief Justice, shoving his fat ass into the town tennis court. "They are coming! Go on! The damned Martians are coming!" the mob repeated their inane exclamation.

"Order in the court! Order in the court!" the Chief Justice was shouting like an absolute lunatic and avid tennis fan.

Going northward during the wild carriage ride, upon the road which paralleled the Great Northern Railway, my mentally-disheveled brother and his two lady passengers looked ahead, and the trio immediately realized that the normally bustling station was in total shambles, and that no trains were operating upon the tracks. At least a dozen dead bodies had been randomly strewn all about the main entrance to the seemingly abandoned platform.

"This is absolutely horrible!" Dorothy frightfully cried to Har. "You' say that you're a damned undertaker! What the hell could you do about this morbid carnage?"

"The dozen deceased souls are deader than mournful Moses; than jaded Judas Iscariot; than that heretic Henry the VIII, and even deader than that mythological meathead, Methuselah!" totally upset Mrs. Elphinstone sobbingly and candidly remarked. "This surreal scenario is much worse than my untamed evening riding horse, mercurial Molly, that happens to be a veritable night mare!"

"Ladies," Harry grimly began summarizing. "I do believe that those dozen dead corpses lying and rotting at the station's entrance have all suffered traumatic, terminal illnesses!"

Chapter 17

"THE THUNDER CHILD"

As Harry drove the chaise onward, pulled by Dorothy's pony, Dolly, over rural street bumps to a quieter stretch of road, Mrs. Elphinstone told a fairly bizarre story about how her daughter had lost her virginity.

"Two months ago, I suggested that Dottie should go into the family barn and take a ride on Dolly to get some nightly fresh air and also some exercise for the pony. Instead," Mrs. Elphinstone continued, "Dottie jumped on Molly, my nasty-tempered equine."

"I thought you had said Molly," Dorothy firmly objected. "You shouldn't bark instructions to me when you're chewing food. You slur your words!"

"I said Dolly, and not Molly," Mrs. Elphinstone corrected, gritting her teeth. "And stop being so damned petulant! Anyway, Harry; Dottie stupidly mounted Molly instead of Dolly, and the wild animal took-off like a bat out of hell, jumping all over the pasture like a berserk maniac. The very wicked up and down impacts upon the hard saddle had busted Dorothy's cherry, and now all of the eligible bachelors in the area think that my precious daughter is damaged goods, and not marriage material!"

"Thanks a lot," Dorothy bitched to her austere mother. "Now, not even my kindergarten boyfriend Buster Cherry will have anything to do with me!"

If the methodical Martians had aimed their goal as solely performing mass destruction, the attackers might have annihilated the entire population of London on Monday. But instead, the vipers concentrated their efforts on destroying the outlying counties.

On *that* spring morning, not only along the road through Barnet, but also on the meandering way through Edgware; through Waltham; through Deer Abbey, in addition, through the lanes going eastward to

Southend; and also, the territory south of the Thames to Deal and Broadstairs, the same frantic rout of displaced, nomadic evacuees poured in all directions, everywhere.

Never before in the history of the world, not even in the Old Testament Bible with the great Exodus out of Egypt, had such a huge mass of troubled human beings moved and suffered together so tremendously. The legendary hordes of Goths and Huns, the largest armies Asia has ever seen, would have been but a mere drop of water in comparison to the London area migration.

And this was no disciplined march; it was a fanatical and turbulent stampede of ruffians, without any semblance of order, and without any particular destination; six million people, mostly unarmed and driving headlong, were fighting for food and for faster means of transportation.

In short, at the time, the massive northern migration was the beginning of the vanquishment of mankind's frail and fragile civilization. It is possible that a considerable number of people in London had stayed inside their houses through Monday morning. However, many died at home, suffocated by the contemptible Black Smoke that drenched the metropolitan suburbs.

Tall Martian mobile forts appeared in a triangle formation beyond the Clock Tower, and were wading waist-deep down the Thames. And the result of their all-powerful weaponry was a plethora of river wreckage floating above Lemonhouse and also near Limehouse.

The sixth cylinder fell and crashed at Wimbledon, right in the middle of the famous Croquet and Lawn Tennis Club. Harry, keeping watch beside the two ladies who were resting in the chaise, parked in a secluded meadow, and soon observed the flashing green streak of a new meteor's descent far beyond the hills.

On Tuesday, the three-person-party, still set upon getting to the North Sea, made their way towards Colchester, evading hostile refugees on the prowl whenever necessary. The news that the non-stoppable Martians were now in possession and control of the whole of London was confirmed from wandering stragglers, again and again. The adversaries' shiny machines. and their green and white "demolition rays", had been seen at Highgate, and even maneuvering-around at Neasden.

That day, the London piers, telegraph lines, and railroads had mostly been exploded into smithereens. The scattered multitudes began to realize the urgent need of obtaining essential life provisions. As the migrating masses grew hungrier and hungrier, the rights of property ownership ceased to be sanely regarded. Trigger-happy farmers were out to defend their cattle-sheds, granaries, and ripening root crops, brandishing loaded shotguns and pistols in their hands.

A number of people, like my brother Harry, had their faces and legs pointed eastward, and there were some desperate souls even considering going back towards London to attempt obtaining food. Har had heard that about half the members of the government had gathered at Birmingham, and that enormous quantities of high explosives were being prepared to be used in mines to be set across the Midland counties.

There was also a hand-scribbled placard in Chipping Ongar announcing that large supplies of flour were available in the northern towns, and that within twenty-four hours, bread would be distributed among the starving, on-the-move population. But this intelligence did not deter the soon-to-be-mortician from the basic escape plan he had formulated, and the three itinerants pressed eastward all day, and heard no more prattle or drivel of the "government bread dissemination program" than the aforementioned vague, gossiped distribution.

That night, the ninth awesome cylinder (I believe) fell upon Primrose Hill. The interplanetary meteor crashed while Dorothy was alertly watching the night sky as a reliable lookout, for she took that duty seriously, alternating with my brother.

On Wednesday, the three unscathed fugitives had reached Chelmsford, and there, a volunteer body of the town inhabitants, calling themselves the Committee of Public Supply, seized the pony, and would give nothing in exchange for Dolly except the promise of a share in its meat the next day.

"Poor Dolly," Mrs. Elphinstone commented as the three fugitives sat around a small campfire. "She'll be missed. If I recall, Dolly had been imported from America, and my husband George claimed that her ancestors had been part of the western Pony Express."

"I loved Dolly, almost as a member of our family," Dorothy admitted and sniffled. "I refuse to eat any flesh from her carcass, regarding such activity as being a form of cannibalism, no matter how hungry I might be!"

"I'll do the same out of respect to you," Harry declared. "For the short time I knew her, I really liked that obedient and loyal animal, it behooves me to say."

People were watching for Martians from the myriad church towers spread all across southern England. My determined brother preferred to push-on at once to the east coast, rather than wait for promised rationed food. Har convinced his traveling companions to ignore their hunger and move-on to finally reach permanent safety.

By midday, the footsore trio passed through Tillingham, which, strangely enough, seemed to be quite silent and deserted, save for a few furtive scavengers scrounging-around for edibles. Two days later, the three then gratefully came in sight of the eastern sea, and the most amazing crowd of nautical shipping vessels, of all sizes, were anchored offshore.

"We're now about seventy or so miles northeast of London," Harry noted. "This is around where the English Channel meets the North Sea!"

"Look at all the idle ships," Dorothy indicated with her right index finger. "Please tell me, Mr. Wells. Do you have two brothers named Oil and Water?" Dottie joked and flirted.

"That was very punny," Harry replied. "Actually, it was two-thirds of a pun; p-u!"

"Sailors are bringing people onto this coast from London and other affected cities and towns," the young lady noted, turning serious. "The Martian invasion must be for real to create all of this elevated activity."

"Right!" my brother replied and agreed. "With all of this destruction that the octopus-like Martians are causing, who knows how many billions of squid it will cost to rebuild everything!"

"Not only English ships and sailors," all-too-sophisticated Mrs. Elphinstone snobbishly contributed, not acknowledging Har's pathetic sense of humor. "The ships and yachts have flags representing Scotland, Sweden, Holland, and France, all evidently working in concert to rescue shocked British nomads from the maniacal Martian scourge."

"No joking around," Harry reminded his female companions. "The Martians have done what the world could never accomplish; they've brought different countries into an alliance of mutual survival in order to help and assist one another."

About a mile out in the open sea lay a fabulous ironclad, very low in the water, indicating a huge load of weighty cargo being carried aboard. This remarkable ram was the famous *Thunder Child,* which had been at the moment, the only close-by warship in sight.

The remainder of the impressive ironclads in the notorious Channel Fleet could be seen steaming a full two miles distant up the coast, preparing for action, and the armada's presumed assignment being to guard the Thames Estuary, which was vital for shipping essential commerce into the port of London.

"Oh dear, Harry," Mrs. Ethel Elphinstone remarked to my one and only sibling. "I've never before been out of England, and I fear that the quarrelsome French, the Belgians, or the Dutch might be just as intolerant of me as would be the callous Martians."

"The French, the Belgians, or the Dutch might mock or ridicule you, but they would *not* exterminate you as if you were a pesty roach or spider."

"I want to go back to my home in Stanmore," Ethel cried aloud. "I immensely miss my library and my dear husband. And I've always been so patriotically British that I doubt whether I can successfully assimilate into another culture and master another language. I suppose I'm just too ethnocentric and spoiled, and I'm falsely believing that England is superior to all other nations!"

"Don't be surprised if you discover that a week from now, if you're still alive," Har qualified, "that your cherished library and your doctor husband have been vaporized by one of the Martian omnipotent rays."

"Usually, dear mother; you speak bullshit; sometimes horseshit; and once in a while chicken shit," Dorothy criticized her opinionated parent. "But now, you're positively talking insignificant mouse shit!"

It was with the greatest difficulty that the three descended a short cliff and skidded-down a sandy dune to the beach, where waving furiously for five minutes, Harry succeeded in attracting the attention of several men standing on the deck of a merchant marine steamer that had been temporarily anchored. The astute captain sent a small rescue boat to the shore, and my brother negotiated a bargain of thirty-six pounds, the sum being paid to conduct the three passengers to Ostend.

"Where's Ostend?" Ethel asked and demanded knowing. "I've studied and learned my geography, and Ostend certainly isn't in England."

"Ostend is in Belgium," Dorothy proudly answered. "I learned that simple fact in sixth grade."

"Great!" Harry exclaimed. "We might not know the language, or the culture, but we can certainly enjoy eating plenty of Belgian waffles and Brussels sprouts!"

Already, there were scores of escaping British passengers crammed aboard the steamer, some of whom had expended their last bit of money. The captain would probably have remained longer to salvage more paying evacuees had it not been for the sound of heavy artillery that started booming toward the south.

The nearby ironclad fired a small gun signal, and the naval crew hoisted a string of flags. Quickly, a jet of smoke sprang-out of her massive funnels, and the heavy anchor was swiftly hoisted.

Far away to the southeast, the paddlewheel's officers and passengers were stunned to witness the masts and decks of three ironclads rise out of the sea, the phenomenon happening beneath clouds of black smoke.

Corresponding with that quick nautical devastation being schemed by the plotting Martian machines, Harry's keen attention speedily reverted to the distant firing occurring to the south. My perceptive brother fancied he saw an immense column of smoke rising-out of the distant grey haze.

The little steamer was already flapping her rear paddles eastward of the big shipping lane, where freighters regularly traversed between mainland Europe and England, and the low Essex Coast was growing blue and hazy. When coincidentally, a contemptible Martian machine appeared upon the southern horizon, at first small and faint in the remote distance; but still, the menace adamantly advancing along the muddy coast from the direction of Foulness.

At *that* sighting, the merchant steamship captain standing upon the bridge swore at the top of his voice with fear and anger, cursing his own delay at moving earlier out to sea. Every soul aboard the old paddlewheel stood at the bulwarks, or upon the steamer's seats, and stared at that distant alien shape, higher than the trees, or taller than the inland coastal church towers. And the Martian threat was advancing with a purposeful stride, as if warfare was merely a mild form of child's play.

"We might as well start praying," Ethel suggested in a defeated tone of voice. "I saw the pallid look on the captain's harrowed face. In truth, we don't stand an icicle's chance of survival inside a hot blast furnace!"

"If we can make it past that landmark jetty up ahead, the Belgium shore should soon be visible and attainable!" Harry informed. "There's a North Sea map on the wall just inside that shows our exact location relative to Ostend."

"Let's think positive! Forget about Brussels sprouts, but instead, think about delicious Belgian waffles wonderfully smothered in delectable maple syrup," Dorothy commented to her distressed mother.

It was the first Martian walking-fort my brother had ever seen close-up, and Har stood by the vessel's railing, more amazed than terrified, watching that mammoth Titan slowly and deliberately pacing towards the established shipping lanes, and soon, wading further and further into deeper water.

Then, far away beyond the Crouch, came another tremendous twin to the first mechanism, striding over some stunted trees, and then yet a third machine, still farther off, wading deeply through a shiny mudflat. It was then that Harry accurately theorized that the invading Martian vehicles operated in groups of three.

The obdurate and heartless alien units were all stalking their various prey seaward, as if to intercept and eliminate the myriad salvage ships that were crowded with refugees who were passengers sailing between Foulness and Walton-on-Naze, which was situated on the east coast of Essex, jutting-out into the North Sea.

In spite of the throbbing exertions of the strained engines motoring the small steamboat, along with the pouring foam that her wheels flung behind her at full throttle, the *Perils of Fate* receded with terrifying slowness from the ominous alien pursuit.

Much to Har's relief, the nearest metallic monster, seeking larger targets to disintegrate, had turned around and was soon wading north. Looking in *that* direction, the renowned torpedo ram, namely *Thunder Child*, steaming headlong, was coming to the rescue of the threatened ships transporting the apprehensive British passengers to various towns and cities on the European side of the North Sea.

Keeping his footing on the heaving deck by clutching the bulwarks, my brother again looked past the charging naval leviathan, and peered at the approaching Martians. And Har perceived the three new Martian forts, with their wading tripod legs, then almost-entirely submerged up to their shoulders.

Thus, the *Thunder Child* fired no guns, but simply drove full-speed-ahead towards the three lethal enemy machines. It was probably the navy beast's commander deciding not to fire first that enabled the battleship to get so near the dreaded enemy as she did. If an errant shell had blasted toward the nearest shiny machine, then the insidious Martian mobile fort would have sent the pride of the Royal Navy straight to the sea bottom, utilizing the inimitable Heat-Ray, White Beam, or Black Tube.

Suddenly, the foremost Martian apparatus lowered its long black tube and discharged a quantity of gas at the approaching ironclad. Amazingly, the fantastic tube's solid projectile glanced off the *Thunder Child's* starboard side, which instantly emitted an inky jet fluid that rolled-away onto the sea, and immediately, unleashed a thick torrent of Black Smoke, from which the ironclad fortunately drove clear.

To the awed spectators standing on the paddlewheel's deck, being low in the water and with the sun in their eyes, it seemed as though the best of the navy's battleships had already-been-engaged in fierce battle among the soul-less Martian enemy.

One of the wading machines raised its camera-like generator, which was creatively designed to emit the formidable Heat-Ray. The firing instrument held the barrel pointing obliquely downward, and a bank of dense steam sprang from the sea at its very activation. The arcane ray astonishingly drove through and penetrated the thick iron plates of the battleship's port side, penetrating its density like a white-hot rod piercing through paper.

Harry, Ethel and Dorothy stood in awe as the *Thunder Child's* huge guns sounded through the reek, going-off one after the other, and one errant shot splashed the water high into the air, landing close by their fleeing and still-vulnerable escape steamer.

"We might be blown to bits as mere collateral damage," Harry loudly shouted to his lady friends above the ear-shattering gun blasts. "The bastard Martians aren't specifically aiming for us, but we stand to be impacted just by being on the fringe of the raging battle!"

"Two Martian units are down!" yelled the excited captain. "The *Thunder Child's* taking the fight to the raunchy sons-of-bitches! Oh; sorry ladies," the ranking officer of the *Perils of Fate* hollered as he realized that Ethel and Dorothy had overhead his inadvertent colloquial slang."

"That's perfectly okay," Dorothy yelled in the embarrassed captain's ear. "I've heard a lot worse foul language in the girl's lavatory at school!"

The odd steam from the black tube hung upon the sea for many minutes, hiding the third Martian juggernaut, which had been the closest one to the Essex Coast. And all that time, the dependable steamboat, reminiscent of one from Mark Twain's Mississippi River era, was paddling steadily out to sea, away from the brutal fight; and when at last the great confusion had cleared, the drifting bank of black vapor intervened, and nothing of the *Thunder Child* could be distinctly made-out, nor could the third Martian fortress be seen.

But the other ironclads at sea were now quite close, and moving inward towards the shore, speeding past Harry's surviving "Mississippi steamboat", with its dual smoke stacks eddying an abundance of carbon into the atmosphere, the *Perils of Fate* had been miraculously spared, and was destined for salvation.

"Thank God!" Ethel marveled and sighed. "I think we'll make it safely to Belgium, after all. My only hope is that my husband is still alive. Frankly, I'm through with greedily pursuing materialism! I don't care if my home is still standing! I'm just glad to be breathing, and in my mind, besides dear Dorothy still being alive, that's all that really matters!"

"Ditto, Mother Dearest!" Dorothy concurred with a smile. "We can go to the British embassy and borrow enough money for food, shelter, and transportation back to England, and together, we'll start new lives."

"With a little imagination," interrupted Har, "I can taste those scrumptious Belgian waffles right now. Forget the damned Brussels sprouts. Pass the butter and the delicious maple syrup!"

* * * * * * * * * * * *

Thankfully, the *Perils of Fate* had made a safe voyage across the North Sea from the Essex Coast to Ostend. Cooperative Belgian government officials mercifully transported Ethel, Dorothy and Harry to the British Embassy in Amsterdam, where the three survivors were provided with food vouchers, and were assisted with moderate living accommodations in a fairly decent city apartment complex.

A month later, after enjoying a side excursion to tour historic Antwerp, the three acquaintances returned to Amsterdam and immediately learned some fabulous news. The Martians had been wonderfully vanquished all over England, which apparently, was the first and only country to be malevolently invaded and systematically decimated.

The British Embassy contacted Harry's bank in London, which amazingly, was still standing, operational, and doing business. A thousand pounds was conveniently wired from England to an Amsterdam financial institution, and then Har had sufficient funds to get back to England and pay-off his "IOU debts" to Belgium for that country's courteous hospitality and stellar welfare benefits, which had been generously and graciously provided to my brother, and to many other British refugees.

Ethel and Dorothy experienced similar good fortune with finances being transferred from British to Belgian banks, and a week later, the three evacuees boarded a ferry at Zeebrugge, which traversed the choppy English Channel over to Dover, where the famous White Cliffs were a welcome sight for the three jubilant passengers to behold.

On the ferry ride back to "the Kingdom", Harry and his female companions learned from newspaper accounts that venerable Buckingham Palace; the invaluable Crown Jewels at the Tower of London; majestic Big Ben, along with the prestigious House of Parliament, had all miraculously escaped major Martian devastation.

However, the Tower Bridge had been severely damaged, and the fabled London Bridge was falling-down in several sections, and plans are currently being devised for the historic spans to be reconstructed. Several auditoriums in the popular theater district had also been destroyed, but Piccadilly Circus is now regaining its tourist-friendly, carnival atmosphere.

Unfortunately, in terms of extremely negative news, the dome atop St. Paul's Cathedral had collapsed after being scorched by the destructive green Heat-Ray; Kensington Palace had been vaporized, and hundreds of bad-luck citizens trying to hide inside Hyde Park had been heinously disintegrated by the alien's formidable White Beam.

However, the London tabloids, prone to hyperbole, printed that Martians had conducted one rather interesting experiment at the Royal Family's Frogmore Cottage, where the native amphibious frogs were joined hopping on land by odd-looking Martian versions of horned toads and newts.

As far as the major cities, spread-out across the Kingdom are concerned, the Queen intends to replace leveled Kensington Palace with a new castle in Newcastle, while most of the northern metropolises had experienced extensive damage: especially Glasgow, Coventry, Edinburgh, Sheffield, and Leeds.

Many confused residents are moving from York, Manchester, Birmingham, and Derby. and especially relocating in New York, New Hampshire, Alabama, and Kentucky, besides voluntarily leaving, by ocean steamers, for New England, New Haven, and New London, respectively.

On the positive side, my wife Beatrice's Leatherhead cousins, Dubious Doug and Doubting Thomas, are presently in the midst of rebuilding their partially collapsed soccer ball factory, and the obnoxious dipshits are adding a new wing to begin production of an expensive line of leather rugby balls, too.

Liverpool had also experienced incredibly-collapsed infrastructure such as roads, tunnels and bridges, in addition to numerous disintegrated downtown structures. And optimistically, brand new construction supplies are being hastily delivered by every available barge and ferry across the Mersey.

A new militant sheriff has been installed to replace the deceased, highest police officer in Nottingham, and the best news of all, the adults, along with the kids in Bristol are still sharp as a pistol, because the Martians didn't do, a Bristol stomp.

Now that I've arrived back home and am authoring this comprehensive account, a full month later, I've learned some essential information from reliable sources about certain important people in my life.

As for my traumatized wife Beatrice, my off-the-wall spouse had deliriously wandered-off into oblivion while we were trekking north, and her fate is still unknown. Army Private Henry Morgan also had abandoned my company in the forest north of Maybury Hill, and has mysteriously disappeared out of my life. And I read in a London newspaper that the chubby curate had undergone a brief rehabilitation conducted at St. Mary's of Bethlehem Mental Hospital II, after the chunky cleric had experienced tremendous bedlam, and astonishingly, after also suffering another major emotional breakdown inside Winchester Cathedral. Ironically, Bartholomew Nicholas Aloysius Murdoch is now the authentic Archbishop of Winchester, since no other sane or insane priest or minister wanted any part of *that* ignoble responsibility.

After I had arrived back to Maybury Hill from my challenging travels and misadventures, I was greatly flabbergasted to see that my humble cottage was still intact. A week later, my brother Har paid me a surprise visit and related that he was going to marry Dorothy, right after his expected graduation from the London Mortuary College.

Ethel Elphinstone's dedicated doctor husband George had retreated from their residence in Stanmore, and had swiftly escaped the Martians to neighboring Epsom, where the elderly surgeon had starved and froze to death while hiding inside a deserted salt mine.

And Harry and Dorothy will join Ethel and me in a joint wedding ceremony to be officiated by Archbishop Bartholomew Nicholas Aloysius Murdoch in a tiny-but-quaint Swindon chapel. Even though Ethel is fifteen years older than myself, I've come to realize that I prefer prudish, Puritanical, aristocratic women, who abhor pornography magazines, and who wholly despise abnormal and gross sexual activity.

In the end, according to Oxford and Cambridge University science department reports, the evil Martians had perished, because the overconfident reptilians had been vulnerable to the countless microbes that inhabit the precious Earth's atmosphere, which human life, over the eons, had developed special immunity to the myriad germs, that in the end, were truly alien and lethal to the inhuman alien invaders.

About the Author

Jay Dubya is author John Wiessner's pen name. John is a retired New Jersey public school teacher, having diligently taught the subject for thirty-four years. John lives in Hammonton, New Jersey.

Counting *Poe: Pelted, Pounded, Pummeled and Pulverized*, John has written and published sixty-two total books. *Pieces of Eight, Pieces of Eight, Part II, Pieces of Eight, Part III* and *Pieces of Eight, Part IV* all contain short stories and novellas that feature science fiction and paranormal plots and themes. *Nine New Novellas, Nine New Novellas, Part II, Nine New Novellas, Part III, Nine New Novellas, Part IV, One Baker's Dozen, Two Baker's Dozen, Snake Eyes and Boxcars* and *Snake Eyes and Boxcars, Part II* are short story collections all written in the spirit of the *Pieces of Eight* series.

Other Jay Dubya adult-oriented fiction are the works *Black Leather and Blue Denim, A '50s Novel*, and its exciting sequel, *The Great Teen Fruit War, A 1960' Novel. Frat Brats, A '60s Novel* completes the action/adventure trilogy. Jay Dubya also has produced two irreverent Biblical satires, *The Wholly Book of Genesis* and *The Wholly Book of Exodus*. A third satire *Ron Coyote, Man of La Mangia* is a parody on Miguel Cervantes' classic novel, *Don Quixote* published in 1605. *Thirteen Sick Tasteless Classics, TSTC, Part II, TSTC, Part III* and *TSTC, Part IV* are satirical works that each corrupt thirteen classic stories from American and British literature and from Greek mythology. *Fractured Frazzled Folk Fables and Fairy Farces* and *FFFF & FF, Part II* satirize and corrupt famous children's literature stories. *Mauled Maimed Mangled Mutilated Mythology* is another popular adult-oriented satirical/parody work that pokes fun at twenty-one famous classical myths. *O. Henry: Obscenely and Outrageously Obliterated* is another satirical adult rewrite. Finally, *Shakespeare: Slammed, Smeared, Savaged and Slaughtered* and *Shakespeare: S, S, S and S. Part II* poke fun at the famous works of the great playwright.

The author has also penned a young adult fantasy trilogy: *Pot of Gold, Enchanta* and *Space Bugs, Earth Invasion. The Eighteen Story*

Gingerbread House is a collection of eighteen new children's stories. And last but not least, two non-fiction works are *So Ya' Wanna' Be A Teacher* and *Random Articles and Manuscripts*.

Jay Dubya really likes '50s music and he also listens to songs by the Beatles, *ELO*, the Carpenters, the Beach Boys, Fleetwood Mac, the Eagles', the Rolling Stones, John Mellencamp and John Fogerty.

Author Biography

Born in Hammonton, NJ in 1942, John Wiessner had attended St. Joseph School up to and including Grade 5. After his family moved from Hammonton to Levittown, Pa in 1954, John attended St. Mark School in Bristol, Pa. for Grade 6, St. Michael the Archangel School in Levittown for Grades 7 and 8 and then Immaculate Conception School, Levittown, Pa. for Grade 9. Bishop Egan High School, Levittown Pa was John's educational base for Grades 10 and 11, and later in 1960, the aspiring author graduated from Edgewood Regional High, Tansboro, NJ. John then next attended Glassboro State College, where he was an announcer for the school's baseball games and also read the nightly news and sports over WGLS, GSC's radio station.

John Wiessner had been primarily an English teacher in the Hammonton Public School System for 34 years, specializing in the instruction of middle school language arts. Mr. Wiessner was quite active in the Hammonton Education Association, serving in the capacities of Vice-President, building representative and finally, teachers' head negotiator for 7 years. During his lengthy teaching career, John had been nominated into "Who's Who Among American Teachers" three times. He also was quite active giving professional workshops at schools around South Jersey on the subjects of creative writing and the use of movie videos to motivate students to organize their classroom theme compositions.

John Wiessner was very active in community service, being a past President of the Hammonton Lions Club, where he also functioned for many years as the club's Tail-Twister, Vice-President and Liontamer. John had been named Hammonton Lion of the Year in 1979 and in 2009 received the prestigious Melvin Jones Fellow Award, the highest honor a Lion can receive.

John also was a successful businessman, starting with being a Philadelphia Bulletin newspaper delivery boy for two years in the late 1950s in Levittown, Pennsylvania. After his family moved back to New Jersey in 1959, John worked at his grandparents and his parents' farm markets, Square Deal Farm (now Ron's Gardens in Hammonton) and Pete's Farm Market in Elm, respectively. He later managed his wife's parents' farm market, White Horse Farms in Elm for three summers.

Also, in a business capacity, for 16 summers starting in 1966 John Wiessner had co-owned Dealers Choice Amusement Arcade on the Ocean City, Maryland boardwalk and also co-owned the New Horizon Tee-Shirt Store for eight summers (1973-'81) on the Rehoboth Beach, Delaware boardwalk. In addition, "Jay Dubya" was a co-owner of Wheel and Deal Amusement Arcade, Missouri Avenue and Boardwalk, Atlantic City. And then, for 18 summers beginning in 1986, John had been the Field Manager in charge of farm crew-leaders for Atlantic Blueberry Company (the world's largest cultivated blueberry farm), both the Weymouth and Mays Landing, New Jersey Divisions.

After retiring from teaching in 1999, writing under the pen name Jay Dubya (his initials), John Wiessner became the author of 62 books in the genre Action/Adventure Novels, Sci-Fi/Paranormal Story Collections, Adult Satire, Young Adult Fantasy Novels and Non-Fiction Books. His books exist in hardcover, in paperback and in popular Kindle and Nook e-book formats.

In January of 2022, John Wiessner (Jay Dubya) was nominated into Marquis Who's Who in America, and in April of that same year, was one of nine distinguished Who's Who in America members honored with Lifetime Achievement Awards, all nine sharing an article of recognition appearing in the Wall Street Journal.

Google: Jay Dubya books
Google: Walmart, Jay Dubya